WEB

ELIZABETH PARKER

WEB

ELIZABETH PARKER

First published in London, 2018

ISBN
978-1-9998152-5-7

**TAMARiND HiLL
.PRESS**

Chapter 1

The bell rang, an ear-splitting sound cutting the crisp silence that was heavy in the air of the school hallways. The corridors came to life with students rushing out of classrooms, their lively chatter filling the atmosphere. It was like every single Friday afternoon at San Christo High School. Students couldn't wait to go home and relax, grateful for the weekend break. No one realized that today was different. This was The Day. The day, that would set in motion events that would bring a change in the lives of several people living in this small town.

Angela Hernandez slammed her locker door shut and breathed a sigh of relief. She could finally leave the heavy textbooks behind and enjoy a relaxing weekend. She didn't have any homework; at least, she didn't think she had. Angela was never the one for organization. Like the other students in the school, she had been given a planner at the beginning of the year, but she never used hers. Come to think of it, she wasn't even sure where it was; probably at the bottom of a drawer somewhere. Her organizational skills - or the lack thereof – were often the source of trouble for Angela, as she rarely remembered to do the assignments given to her. However, apart from this tiny issue, Angela was a good student.

As she walked towards the door leading out of the school, she was joined by her friend Kylie. "So, you didn't get overloaded with homework or anything, did you? Nothing disastrous happened?"

"No," Angela pushed open the heavy glass door and moved out into the school courtyard, before turning to look at Kylie with a confused expression on her face. "Why?"

"Well, I was just wondering if you would like to come for a sleepover this Saturday. My parents said that I could have one." She paused for a second, looked in another direction and then smirked. "Well, unless of course you're invited to their party."

Angela followed Kylie's path of vision and saw a group of students from their year group standing in a close circle laughing. She recognized them immediately: anyone in the school would. This was the 'popular' group; the group that everyone knew and secretly, or not-so-secretly, wanted to be part of. These were the kids who were perfect in every way possible. They had perfect physical features – perfect hair that never frizzed, perfect eyes that didn't require vision correction, and perfect teeth that never needed braces. They were talented too, not only getting brilliant grades, but excelling at the extra-curricular activities that their school offered. Ever since Angela had started secondary school, she yearned to be a part of their 'exclusive clique'. She wanted to be someone whom everybody knew, looked up to, compared themselves to and someone they even wanted to be. Of course, she wanted to go to the legendary parties thrown by the in-crowd. According to the rumor mill, Mitzi - the tall, sporty blonde that everyone adored - was having a party at her house tomorrow night. Her parents were out of town and it was going to be "Lit", as Angela had heard someone put it. However, the invitees' list only included the popular kids and anyone they could bear to associate with, and much to her chagrin, Angela did not meet the requirements.

"I wish I was," Angela said, a tinge of longing in her voice. Kylie raised an eyebrow, and Angela quickly said, "But, even if I was, I would totally ditch them and come to yours." Kylie didn't look convinced, so Angela changed the subject. "So... who's coming to your place anyway? Who'd you invite?"

"Oh, you know, the usual," Kylie waved her hand around in the air. "You, Jordyn, Summer and -," she was interrupted by a voice in the background.

"Angela! Angela!"

Kylie's face contorted into a disgusted expression. "And I certainly did not invite her."

Angela swivelled around to see who Kylie was talking about now. She spotted a girl with black hair that was tightly tied back into a ponytail, grey-green eyes that were obstructed by glasses with thick black frames and skin with a dodgy complexion. She was running towards them and judging by the fact that her face resembled an overly ripe tomato, she had clearly been running for quite a long time. She slowed down as she approached Angela and Kylie, her hands falling to her knees as she bent down and gasped for air.

"Angela!" her voice was raspy. "Angela, thank goodness I caught you! We need to talk!"

Angela raised an eyebrow in reply, before turning away and continuing to walk. The girl, however, continued to chase her. "Angela!"

By now, the girl's loud exclamations had attracted the attention of most people in the courtyard, including that of the 'in-crowd'. They had turned around, interested in what was probably going to make exciting gossip for days to come. Angela suddenly felt the unease, that one feels when all eyes are suddenly focused on them. At that moment, she knew that her reaction would determine how people regarded her, and how people thought of her. This was a make-or-break moment. Taking a deep breath, she turned around again to face the breathless and desperate girl.

"What do you want?" she demanded. The ferocity of her voice made the girl shrivel up slightly, afraid of the confrontation.

"Um, well, I just wanted to know..." she stuttered, "We're paired together for the Biology project that's due on

Monday - you know, the poster on cell respiration. So I just wanted to know whether you're free this weekend so that maybe we could work on it or something?"

Angela froze. She'd forgotten all about the Biology poster. The idyllic image of her weekend vanished, as she tried to figure out what she should do. She knew that she should talk to the girl, divide the work for the project between them and then organize a time to meet up during the weekend, so that they could put it all together. Angela was about to suggest this, when she felt the heat of everybody's eyes on her. She could feel the calculating stare of the clique that she had always wanted to be in. She was presented with the ultimate opportunity, the audition of a lifetime. Being nice to this girl wasn't going to help move her up in the social hierarchy of high school. In fact, it would probably bring her down. Knowing this, she pushed aside her conscience. "I'm busy this weekend," she spoke clearly and loudly, so that everybody could hear what she had to say. "I have a party to go to and I'm not about to be bogged down by a stupid Biology poster. Plus, I definitely do not want to work with you, so I suggest that you do the poster yourself."

She turned and walked away before the girl could say anything. A surprised Kylie followed and said, "Here, I thought you didn't have a mean bone in your body."

Out the corner of her eye, she saw Mitzi smile and she was sure she had passed the test. She felt proud, pushing away the guilt that was left over from the spiteful things she'd just said to the girl, until there was none left. She felt as if it had all been worth it. She might have actually passed the test.

The girl quietly sat down on a bench, sighing to herself. Students who had watched the scene had moved away, in search of another conflict to entertain themselves or simply re-engaging in what they were doing prior. She was forgotten yet again. She knew she was an easy target, with the fact that she had a huge fear of confrontation and was therefore unable to lash back when she was picked on. She was the quiet girl, the one with no friends to defend her and a lonely target, always easy to catch. They laughed at her British accent, still strong having only moved to America from England a few months ago. They laughed at the fact that she always had her nose buried in a book, and at the fact that she actually cared about grades. They laughed at her and she had no defense, slowly shrinking away until she could barely be seen; only two white irises in a sea of darkness.

She opened her shoulder bag that was resting next to her on the bench. It was bright pink, a color that she had chosen because she wanted it to stand out, and stand out it did, but for all the wrong reasons. Here, bright pink was a color that you would see more frequently in the halls of an elementary school and not a high school. High school was a monotonous place with the colors all being varying shades of neutral black, grey, white or navy. Bright pink was like an offense, definitely not a "grown-up" colour. It didn't fit in. It reminded her that she didn't fit in.

From her bag, she extracted a small, patterned notebook. It had a lock on it, so that in case anyone else happened to chance on it, they wouldn't be able to open it and obtain any more ammunition to use against her. The key was kept on the tiny silver charm bracelet that she always wore. She unlocked the notebook and opened it up to the first page. Two words were written in pink glitter pen. "Diana's Journal". She smiled at her book. She often wondered whether or not people knew her name. To many, she was just the 'new girl'. She rarely ever heard anyone refer to her by name unless it was to taunt her, and therefore during the hours she spent in school, she often felt her sense of identity vanish. Thankfully, she'd found that all she needed to regain it was to open up her journal - her object of comfort.

She opened to the first available blank page, took out a pen from her pocket and began to write. In her neat, cursive script, she detailed the confrontation between her and Angela. She had thought Angela was a nice girl, someone who would perhaps understand her and want to be friends with her. She was relieved when she found out they were partners for the project and hadn't expected that Angela would treat her just like everybody else did. But then again, she didn't really know her.

The issue of the Biology project was still outstanding and Diana wasn't sure what she should do. She didn't want to get low grades, but she wasn't sure whether or not she should just do it by herself at home. Maybe if she did do it, Angela would feel bad and apologize for her earlier actions. Diana sighed. She seemed to be in a position where she didn't have much of a choice, because if she didn't do the poster, Angela would probably just get angry and therefore, another confrontation would be inevitable. The last thing she wanted was another skirmish.

Finishing off her entry, Diana replaced the cap on her pen, closed and locked her journal, then deposited both items into her bag. She checked her watch and decided that she should probably head home. Getting up from the bench, she began her journey back to her house that was around fifteen minutes away from San Christo High. She set off, expecting to make the journey the same way she did every day - Alone.

Yet, when she was walking through Edmonton's main shopping street, she was joined by another girl and Diana recognized her immediately. Her name was Rose, and she was in Diana's English class. Although Diana didn't like listening to gossip, she had overheard a few students talking about how Rose's friends had recently turned their backs on her, leaving her all alone. Diana didn't know why this had happened, but she assumed it might have had something to do with Rose's body image. She was slightly overweight and was often teased for it.

"Hey!" Rose's voice was bright, sunny and enthusiastic. "You're Diana, right?"

Diana, shocked that someone was talking to her in a kind manner, let alone referring to her by name, took a minute to reply. "Um, Yeah. I'm Diana."

Rose smiled. "I'm Rose! I'm in your English class!"

"I know."

"You're new, right? From England?"

"Yeah."

"That's so awesome! I've always wanted to go to England. It must be really nice there. But hey, it must be so hard for you, starting out in a new place. If you ever want someone to like, show you around or if you need help or anything, you can come and talk to me! I don't mind at all."

Diana was a little taken aback at Rose's sudden niceness. In the two months that she had been at San Christo High,

Rose had never once talked to her. This made Diana suspicious. What if Rose wasn't actually being genuinely nice to her? What if Rose was trying to befriend her, gain her trust and then ditch her in front of the whole school? What if the whole thing was just a ploy to further humiliate her? After all, what did Diana really know about Rose?

"Thanks," she replied quietly. "If I need anything, I'll let you know."

Rose seemed to sense that something was wrong. "Hey," she said. "Listen, I saw what happened outside the school today, with Angela. Don't worry about it, Angela's actually a really nice girl. Once she gets to know you, she'll be fine. She probably just wasn't sure what to do with everyone glaring at her like that. She doesn't really think things through and about how mean everybody else has been...well, it's mainly Mitzi and her group, isn't it? Don't worry about them, they're just jerks. Edmonton's a really friendly place once you get to know it and the people get to know you. School is no different; well except for Mitzi's gang who taunts everyone really."

Diana became more convinced that Rose's friendliness was just a trick. Why would she be describing Edmonton or school as a friendly place when she'd just lost all of her friends? "Thanks, I'll keep that in mind."

"Do you want to go and get an ice cream?" Rose asked, a huge smile on her face. "There's this really great place I know. I'm sure you'll like it."

"Thanks, but I can't right now. I have to get home," she offered no further explanation before she hurried off. Rose watched her as she went. She understood people well; she knew that Diana mistrusted her. But she meant no harm - she was genuinely nice. She felt bad for Diana, and as they were both picked on - Rose for being overweight, Diana for being the new girl – she felt as if they were similar, as if she could relate to her. She just wanted to help.

Chapter 2

"I'm home!" Angela called as she closed the heavy wooden door of her villa behind her. It was just past noon on Sunday and she'd returned from Kylie's sleepover, which she had enjoyed thoroughly. They had watched movies and gossiped until almost two in the morning, and the incident with Diana on Friday never even came up. It was almost as if it had been completely forgotten.

Angela lived in a pleasant, peaceful neighborhood, just outside the center of town. Her house was old; it had been built by her great-grandfather's family when they had settled in Edmonton before the Great Depression had struck, and the house had remained in the family's possession. Angela loved the vintage feel of the house. She had already planned that when she was initiated into the popular clique, she would throw an unforgettable themed party in the house. The atmosphere was perfect for a historically themed one.

Angela's mother appeared at the top of the stairs. Many people said that Angela took after Mrs. Hernandez in the looks department, and that was certainly true. They had the same hazel eyes and straight nose, the same skin - although Angela's was currently a little more acne-prone - and the same medium-length brown hair. "Hi honey," she beamed. "Why don't you come upstairs? There's something here that you're going to want to see."

"What?" Angela asked curiously as she walked up the spiral stairway that led to the second floor of her house. The curled black banister was unusually slippery and smooth, meaning that Mrs. Hernandez had spent her morning polishing the floors. As Angela walked up, her mind wandered as to what it was that her mom wanted her to see. Mrs. Hernandez led her into the master bedroom, where Angela's father was waiting. He was sitting on his desk chair, facing the door and his laptop opened behind him. Angela squinted to try and make out the large black letters on the glaring white screen. San Christo High School-Progress Report it read.

Although most schools waited a good three or four months before releasing the first report card, San Christo High was a little different. Two months into the school year, they emailed out 'progress reports' to parents and every month after. Progress reports looked and functioned the same way as normal report cards. They were the instruments of torture that made parents aware of the fact that most of the time, their children were not actually working in school, and messing around instead. Angela's parents, like most others, were incredibly strict about schoolwork and grades. Nervousness began to build up inside her. What if she'd gotten horrible marks?

Her tension was quickly relieved when her father smiled. "We received your report card just a little while ago. Well done Angela! We're very proud of you."

"Straight A's!" Mrs. Hernandez could barely contain her excitement. "Our baby got straight A's!"

"Straight A's?" Angela was incredulous. "Seriously?"

"Well, almost," Mrs. Hernandez conceded. "You got a B in Math, but that's okay. You've never been particularly good at math, so a B is actually excellent for you. But anyway, we are so very proud of you sweetheart."

Angela found herself breaking out into a massive grin. "Wow. I can't believe it!" She knew she'd done well in tests and she had put quite a bit of effort into her essays and major assignments, wanting her freshman year to go as well as possible. However, she had never expected to get straight A's in her report card considering the fact that she hadn't submitted the majority of her small assignments. Even if it was just a progress report, it still counted.

Mrs. Hernandez gave Angela a huge hug. "We've decided that for doing so well, you have to be rewarded!"

"Rewarded?" Angela perked up. She knew people who got money or gifts from their parents every time they got an A. She wasn't one of them. Being an only child, her parents had decided early on that they didn't want to spoil her. Giving her gifts whenever she got good marks constituted as spoiling to them and therefore, they had never established a reward system for Angela. The fact that she would be getting something for doing well in school was a new and exciting prospect for Angela.

Mr. Hernandez opened the first drawer in his wooden desk. Like the house itself, along with most of the furniture, the desk was bought back when furniture items were actually carved and created out of real wood; not the fake, cheap stuff sold nowadays that Mrs. Hernandez refused to buy. He reached inside the drawer and brought his black, leather wallet out. The wallet was not vintage; it's shiny freshness contrasting deeply with the dusty antiquity of the rest of the room. Flipping the wallet open, he took out an American Express card. He got up and handed it to Angela.

"Remember how for your birthday you wanted your own credit card? So you could go shopping online?" he asked Angela, who nodded eagerly in reply. "Well, your mother and I had a discussion, and we've decided that you can use our credit card to make online purchases - of course, as long as they're within reason. Going and buying a twenty-five thousand dollar limited edition Gucci dress or something would be completely out of the question, but you can buy other things like books, cheaper dresses, and games."

Angela laughed. "Don't worry Daddy, I'm not going to do something like that. Thank you so much!" She looked down at the sleek credit card in her hand, running her fingers over the numbers. Holding it gave her a strange sense of power, a sense that was rather hypnotizing. It drew her in.

She broke out of the trance when her father snatched the card from her hand using his index and middle fingers. "We may be allowing you to use the card, but that doesn't mean you can keep it with you. Keeping a credit card IS a lot of responsibility and with your forgetfulness, Angela, you may just lose it. Plus, your mother and I do need to use it."

"Of course," Angela was a little disappointed. She had wanted to show off the credit card to everyone. None of them could use their parents' cards, not even Kylie, who was spoilt rotten by her parents. Angela knew that if she could show everyone the card, she would immediately be promoted to a higher level in the social hierarchy at school. "I'll ask you when I want to use it."

Mrs. Hernandez smiled. "Okay sweetie. Anytime you want it, just come and ask your father or me."

"Of course. Thank you!" Angela walked out of her parents' room, with a smile on her face. Although she couldn't keep the card with her, she was happy that her parents had given her such an extravagant reward. However, it caused her to worry a little bit about the Biology project. She didn't want her grades to drop. She walked into her room, sat down at her desk and opened her MacBook Pro. For a minute, she contemplated whether or not to look up Diana on the school directory. Maybe she should call her and organize something.

But, what if someone got wind of it? Diana was trodden upon by the popular students, the ones that Angela so desperately wanted to be like. If they found out that Angela was talking to Diana, she would receive the same wrath. She couldn't have that, not now that they had acknowledged her and approved of something that she had done, which ironically was being mean to Diana. Angela quickly shook the idea out of her head, because she wasn't going to get bad marks on the Biology project anyway. Diana was too conscious about grades to not do the poster. She'd do it by herself and because she didn't want to become even more of a reject, she wouldn't tell the teacher that Angela didn't do any work. Although they were in high school, the brand of being a 'tattle-tale' was still something that everybody wanted to avoid. Angela sighed thankfully.

She typed her password into her Mac, and her desktop came up. She clicked on the Safari icon and was immediately transported into the internet world. She clicked on the Facebook icon and logged into her account. In Angela's opinion, Facebook was a wonderful way of accelerating her popularity. She had quite a few members of the popular clique as Facebook friends and often liked to scroll through their Timelines to find out what they were doing or where they were going. Once, she had seen that they were at an ice-cream parlor near her house and had then ventured out, 'coincidentally' bumping into them. She also liked all of their photos and statuses, just so that they were aware that she existed. It would also increase the probability that one of her posts would pop up on their homepages.

Angela posted almost everything on Facebook. She posted about what she was doing, where she was going and who she was with. She even posted pictures and videos. Her personal details, such as her full name, date of birth, and even her phone number were all online.

Angela didn't see the harm of putting this information online. Only her friends could see them, right? What she didn't realize was that her Facebook settings were on the "public" option and as such anyone who went onto her profile could see everything that she had posted.

Scrolling down her homepage, she saw that a number of people had posted about their report cards. Some were angry statuses that yelled at the respective persons' parents for grounding them over an F in English or a C in Economics. Others were ecstatic ones over receiving a new MacBook or iPhone for doing so well. Most people had pictures along with statuses. Scrolling further down, Angela saw that Mitzi had received a brand new Retina-display MacBook Pro for getting straight A's. There was a picture of the shiny new laptop that already had several likes, and was acquiring more as time went on. At once, Angela felt the need to post about the privilege that she had been given as a reward.

She went up to the top of the homepage and clicked on the little rectangular space that asked her what was on her mind. The text vanished, and the type cursor materialized. She began to type. "I get to use my parents' credit card whenever I want! Thank you SO much Mom&Dad!" Just as she was about to click 'post', she had an idea. There was no reason she couldn't attach a picture as well. But then again, her parents would never let her. Maybe they didn't need to. Neither of her parents had Facebook, so if she somehow managed to get a quick photo of the card, they would never see it.

Footsteps could be heard going down the stairs, and Angela could hear her parents' voices getting fainter and fainter. She got up from her desk, walked towards the door and tiptoed into her parents' room. There was no one there, so she eased the top drawer of her fathers' desk open and slid her hand in, feeling around until she grasped the wallet. Extracting it, she quickly scampered back to her room, where she flipped the wallet open and took out the card. The plastic felt cold in her hand and she was again filled with the sudden sense of power. This time however, it was more short-lived, as she knew that she was on a clock. She quickly opened PhotoBooth on her laptop and snapped a picture of the card. Then, she placed it back in the wallet and dashed to replace it in her fathers' drawer. When she reached her room again, she uploaded the photo to her status and posted it. A satisfied grin fell across Angela's face and she couldn't wait for everyone to see it.

Angela could hear her mother calling her from downstairs. She closed her laptop and went downstairs, feeling immensely happy with herself.

Meanwhile, Diana had returned home and was sitting alone in her room, feeling horrible about herself. Her sister, Sofia, knocked on the door. Sofia was eighteen years old - three years older than Diana. She had graduated from high school in England and was now attending college just a couple of miles away in a nearby town. Although most graduates would prefer to have their own house and live away from their parents, Sofia had always been incredibly attached to her family. In the summer when her father was transferred to Edmonton, she had been incredibly happy at the prospect of continuing to be close to them, especially Diana, who she was incredibly fond of.

"Diana?" she asked, opening the door slightly. "Are you okay? Would you like something to eat?"

"No thanks," Diana said quietly.

"Hey, what's up?" Sofia came into Diana's room and sat at the foot of the bed. "I'm your sister. You can tell me, no matter what it is and I'll help you out."

"It's nothing really."

"It's not nothing, you seem hurt. Did someone say something?"

"I feel really silly about it, but there's this Biology project that I have to do this weekend and we're supposed to be working in pairs. The girl who I'm to work with – Angela – publicly humiliated me when I asked her when we could work on it. Everyone was watching. She refused to do anything."

"That's so mean! Diana, listen to me. Don't put her name on it. Just do it yourself and don't give her any credit."

"I thought about that, but I can't do that. I don't want her to hate me. Maybe if I do this, she'll decide that she was wrong about me."

Sofia looked doubtful. She didn't want her little sister to get hurt, but it was what she wanted to do and she would have to face the consequences of whatever Sofia would suggest all on her own at school. "Alright then. Dinner will be ready in about half an hour. I'll call you then, okay?"

"Okay."

Later that day, when the inky black shroud of the night had almost completely covered the Earth, someone logged in to Facebook and searched for Angela Hernandez. A Facebook page came up, and the person recognized the face in the profile picture, along with the other pictures that were available on the wall. The person looked at the 'add friend' button before smiling smugly. Who needed to add Angela as a friend when everything was already available to the public?

The person opened a spiral-bound notepad and uncapped a pen. Scrolling through Angela's timeline and information page, this person wrote down everything that was of interest: From when and where she was born, to who her friends were, her phone number, important life events and even the simple things that she liked and disliked. Everything was scribbled down. The person read and wrote, learning everything possible about Angela, everything required to impersonate her.

Once this person was confident about knowing Angela well enough, Facebook was closed and the Twitter homepage opened. On the bottom right corner, there was a box entitled 'New to Twitter? Sign up.' The person wrote Angela Hernandez in the box asking for a full name. A fake email address was input into the email field, in order to avoid detection and also added a simple password - the name of Angela's old puppy that had died several years ago. Upon being redirected to a new page, the person chose the display name of 'angelahernandezxo'. Simple.

After the account had been created and verified, the person got to work. A picture of Angela off her Facebook page was copied and set as the display picture for the Twitter account. A description using the language that Angela used, and including details about Angela was written at the head of the Twitter page. The background of the page was the vintage lily pattern that Angela had posted on Facebook, saying that she had liked it. The person followed the Twitter pages of all of Angela's favorite singers, movie stars and personalities. To anyone who chanced upon the page, it would look as if it was Angela herself who administered the page - but of course it wasn't.

At this stage, the page was harmless and blank, but then, the person investigated further, finding the Twitter handles of several different students in the same school and year as Angela. These handles were then saved in a document on the computer, because they would be incredibly useful as events progressed. A single handle was randomly chosen and a message to this handle was typed out. The person posted the message, feeling incredibly powerful.

Chapter 3

Monday morning came as usual, forcing disinclined students to leave their lazy weekends behind and throwing them headlong into another week of the torture and stress that was high school. The only positive thing about going to school was the opportunity to gossip about the events of the weekend. Naturally, the news item that made the headlines was Mitzi's party. As predicted, it had indeed been wild. Everyone was talking about who was now dating who or who broke up at the party, how everybody jumped into the pool at the very end of the party and ended up walking home dripping wet or just stayed over at Mitzi's house. Naturally, Angela gobbled up every titbit she could get.

She was having a chat about what she had heard about the party with Jordyn, one of Angela's close friends and her mother's best friend's daughter, when she entered sixth-period Biology. They were about to take their usual seats at the back of the class, when Angela spotted Diana. A sudden wave of fear passed through her. What if Diana hadn't done the poster? What if she told on

Angela? Angela had been so sure that Diana would do the work, but what if she hadn't?

She positioned herself so that she could see Diana more clearly. She looked down at the desk in front of Diana and heaved a sigh of relief when she saw a bright orange poster filled with images and information on it. Angela could even see her name written on the bottom right corner, next to Diana's. She looked up again and accidentally caught Diana's gaze. Diana smiled brightly and pointed to the poster. Angela returned her smile with an expression that was somewhere between a grin and a grimace. Diana's face fell.

The rest of the class progressed as normal. When it was time to hand in the posters, Diana silently got out of her chair and placed the large orange sheaf of paper on the teacher's desk. Angela watched this process carefully; afraid that Diana might suddenly change her mind and tell the teacher that Angela hadn't done any work. Thankfully, she immediately returned to her seat after handing the poster in.

It was after class that the two girls came face to face again. Angela was passing Diana's desk on the way to the door, when Diana called out her name. Angela stopped and turned around to face her.

"What do you want?" Angela's tone far from friendly.

As usual, Diana began to shrink back like a mouse. "I just, um, well, I did our poster this weekend and I put a lot of effort into it and I was just wondering whether or not you liked it. I mean, it is your work too." She laughed nervously. "Well, um, not really, but it has your name on it and you'll be graded for it and..."

"It was fine," Angela interrupted abruptly, for no other reason apart from the fact that she just wanted Diana to shut up. However, that did not work. Diana immediately perked up. "Oh, so you liked it? That's great, because I really put quite a lot of effort into it, and I tried to think about what you might've liked to have on it and..."

"When I said it was fine, I meant it was fine," Angela put emphasis on the last word. "I never said that I liked it, I just said that it was fine. Average."

"Oh," Diana glanced at the floor. "Oh! Alright then."

Angela walked off. It was only once she was halfway to the cafeteria to eat lunch that she realized she'd forgotten to say thank you to Diana. After all, the girl had done their entire project all by herself and had still been nice enough to put Angela's name on it. She felt a sudden pang of guilt and was considering turning back when she felt a tap on her shoulder. She swivelled around to see Kylie, who smiled at her. They continued walking on to the cafeteria.

"How was Bio?" Kylie asked. "Did Diana actually do the poster?"

"She did."

"Did she give you any credit?

"Yep. My name was on it and as far as I know, she hasn't said anything to the teacher."

"That's great! Because I realized Angela, it was actually quite a risky thing you did there. I mean, imagine if she didn't do it or if she told on you. You'd be in so much trouble!"

"I know," Angela sighed. They had reached the cafeteria, and headed over to their usual table, near the food lines. They were the last ones to reach and the normal crowd already gathered around the bench. As Angela slid into her chair, the stream of chatter stopped as everyone turned to look at her. This confused her. "Um, hi guys," she said uneasily, unsure what she had done to cause her to be the center of attention. "How's it going?"

"I didn't know you had a Twitter account," Tessie, the girl sitting opposite her, remarked casually.

"I don't..." Angela narrowed her eyes.

"Well, it appears that you do. And you sent a really mean message to Catrine last night, telling her that she's a worthless, dumb blonde. That was really mean of you, Angela!"

"I didn't!" Angela exclaimed. She wasn't sure what everyone was talking about. She certainly did not have a Twitter account and she would never say anything mean to Catrine, the quiet, sensitive girl that she'd known since kindergarten. Catrine was a bit of a loser, but Angela knew that she was a lovely person. She would never want to do anything to hurt her! "It wasn't me. I don't have a Twitter account. It must be another Angela Hernandez."

"Oh no, I'm pretty sure it's you."

"Can you send me the link over Facebook?"

"Fine. I don't see the point of it, since you ought to know the link to your own Twitter page. Just own up to it already."

The minute Angela got home from school, she ran up the stairs, closed the door behind her as she went into her room and opened up her laptop. Opening up Facebook, she saw that she had one new message and clicked on the icon that led her to her inbox. Tessie had sent the link.

Angela clicked on the link and was transported to another webpage. It was clearly a Twitter page which bore the signature bluebird in the corner, and the layout was exactly like all the ones that she had seen before. However, this page didn't bear the picture of a well-known celebrity, nor did it bear the picture of a stranger. She saw her own face, staring back at her from the area allocated for the users' display picture. Diana also saw her own name written across the top, a short description about herself that described where she lived, where she went to school and was written in the same style that she herself wrote in.

She scrolled down the page, taking in everything. The 'following' page showed that whoever had made this page was following all the famous personalities that Angela loved, from Ginnifer Goodwin to Katy Perry. Angela turned her attention to the tweets and the first few were harmless.

First tweet! Yay!

GinnyGoodwin, I think that you're really good in Once Upon A Time! #fairestforever

However, then came the tweet that had caught everybody's attention; with 13 words, a jab was delivered that set the ball rolling. It was a reply to an earlier tweet by Catrine, which was a tearful message about having received a C in History. Angela read the message carefully.

Cat77: well, no surprise there! After all, you're only a worthless, dumb blonde.

Angela looked at it in astonishment. What a mean thing to say! People actually thought that she had said it. Granted, the profile looked exactly like she would style her own, if she had a Twitter page and all of the tweets sounded as if they had been written by her. If she were to write a comment like this, it would be composed in a similar way. Angela couldn't quite accept it as true. She was bewildered by the way someone had managed to crawl into her skin and amazed by the way someone had managed to mimic her so accurately. She had no idea how someone knew so much about her, that they could do such a thing. It scared her.

She knew that she had to tell everyone that it wasn't her Twitter account and that it wasn't her who was writing the messages. That was exactly what she resolved to do tomorrow, because there was a better chance that everyone would believe her if she told them to their faces. Until then, the only thing that she could do was put it out of her mind and concentrate on homework instead; but this was hard.

Chapter 4

That night, Diana was sitting in the living room of her house working on her History essay. She typed furiously, trying to keep her mind on the problems of the Weimar Republic, but she couldn't. She was angry with Angela. Diana had thought that if she did the poster all by herself, it would lead Angela to see her previous mistake and apologize. Maybe they would even become friends, but she was wrong. Instead of apologizing or even thanking her for putting in so much hard work, Angela had turned up her nose and walked off. Diana was furious at her for that and she couldn't even believe that someone could be so arrogant.

At the same time, Diana was angry at herself for being so meek and quiet. She wished that she could stand up for herself, that she could confront people with confidence. The problem is, no matter how hard she tried, she just couldn't and she would always be the tiny mouse who ran away when she came face to face with a cat.

Her train of thought crashed suddenly when she heard a voice behind her say, "what're you doing?" Diana jumped with fright, almost knocking her laptop over. She turned around to see Sofia behind her.

"Oh, it's you," Diana said. "Don't do that, it scared me!"

"Sorry," Sofia put her hands up. She squinted at Diana's face. There was something that was off. Pulling out a chair, she sat down next to Diana. "Hey," she said quietly. "What's up?"

Diana sighed and turned away. "It's nothing."

"Come on love, tell me. Is someone bullying you at school?" Sofia paused for a second, trying to remember previous conversations between the two of them. She remembered the exchange between them about Angela. "Does it have to do with that Angela girl? The girl who refused to do anything on the poster that you spent the entire weekend on?"

"Kind of."

"Di, it's me, okay? If you can't talk to me about it then who can you talk to?"

"Okay, look. I handed in the poster and put her name on it. I asked her if she liked it and she told me that it was average. She just walked away!" Diana shook her head with semi-disgust. "I can't believe she wouldn't even say thank you!"

Sofia looked at Diana's upset face. She couldn't bear to see her sister like this. Sofia had always been incredibly protective and if someone was hurting Diana, she would see to it that it would stop. But right now, she was at a bit of a loss about what to do. So she placed her hand on Diana's shoulder and smiled reassuringly. "Just forget this girl, Di. She clearly isn't worth it. Don't waste your time on someone like that."

Diana smiled. "Thanks Sis. I do appreciate it."

Sofia opened her mouth to say something else, but was interrupted by the shrill sound of Diana's phone ringing. "You should answer that," she said. "I'm sure it's one of your mates calling. Believe me, you'll forget all about Angela soon." She left the room.

Diana reached for the phone and glanced at the screen. She didn't recognize the number, but answered it anyway. "Hiya?"

"Hi, is that Diana?"

"Yea."

"Hi! It's Rose! I got your number off the school directory-I hope you don't mind."

"Um, no, that's okay," Diana was a little unsure as to why Rose was calling her. The girl had seemed very friendly when they had first spoken, but Diana thought that she had made it clear that she didn't exactly want to be friends with Rose. Well, she did want to be friends. It was just that she didn't know whether or not she could trust her.

"Well, I was wondering if you were free this weekend. There's an awesome movie playing down at the cinema, and I'd love it if you could come. It's on Saturday!"

"No thank you," Diana automatically turned the offer down. "I, um, have a lot to do over the weekend."

"Oh, that's unfortunate," Rose sounded legitimately disappointed and Diana went through a moment of doubt, wondering whether or not she should trust Rose and go to the movie. But she shook the idea out of her head quickly - better safe than sorry.

"Thanks for inviting me though. Maybe another time?"

"Yeah, sure. Bye."

"Bye," Diana put the phone down and then turned back to her History essay.

Chapter 5

I will tell everyone that the account isn't mine, Angela thought to herself as she approached the table where her friends were sitting at break time. She could see Tessie glancing at her and then looking away with disgust. It made her feel uncomfortable. *I'll just tell them that it wasn't me and that someone stole my identity. Just like it happens on TV!*

"Hey guys," she casually slid into a chair, ignoring the dirty looks that Tessie was giving her. *I didn't do anything.*

"Did you see the Twitter account?" Tessie asked harshly. "Oh wait, of course you did. After all, it is your account."

"Um, actually Tessie, it..." Angela was interrupted by the sound of high heels clicking against the tiled floor of the cafeteria. The clicking got louder and louder until it came to a stop - right next to Angela. She knew who it was before she looked up. There was only one group of girls who wore heels to school - the popular crowd. She turned her head to look at them and sure enough, she was right. Standing next to her was Mitzi and her crew, looking right at Angela. She couldn't quite believe it, yet she was a little fearful, because she didn't know what she had done to attract their attention and whether or not it was good or bad.

"Angela, right?" Mitzi's voice was smooth and oozing with confidence. By hearing this girl, it was clear that she wasn't fazed by anyone. She was exactly the kind of person Angela wanted to be, cool, yet uncaring.

"Uh..... Yeah," Angela replied, trying to sound as much like Mitzi as she could, but she couldn't help thinking that she sounded like nothing but a desperate copycat. She silently cursed at herself. "I'm Angela," she added, this time in her normal voice.

"We saw the tweet you sent to Clarissa," Mitzi said, looking back at the girls behind her, who immediately nodded when they saw her gaze fall upon them. Angela quickly thought back to when she'd seen the Twitter account yesterday. There had been no tweets to Clarissa, a girl who used to be part of the popular crowd, before she did something that was apparently horrendous. Since then, she had been socially rejected, not just by the popular kids, but by every single kid in the school. Angela knew who she was, but had never spoken to her.

"Actually, the Twitter account isn't..." she began, but was immediately cut off by Mitzi, who held up a palm, and stated, "I wasn't finished."

Angela grew scared. What were they here for? Were they going to get angry at her for coming into contact with Clarissa, who was by all means "outlawed"? What if they outlaw me too? However, her fears went away when she saw Mitzi break out into a smile. "That was sooo amazing and totally cool. I couldn't think it up myself! Shows that you are on our side."

"Oh!" Angela was surprised. "Oh! Yeah. Right. Of course!"

"And that other tweet that you sent to...what's her name?" Mitzi clicked her fingers and looked expectantly back at her entourage who quickly supplied her with the information that she was looking for.

"Cat."

"Oh of course. Cat. Well, that was a stroke of evil genius. Totally cool."

Angela found herself breaking out into a smile. "Thanks."

Mitzi gave Angela a half smile. "I'll see you around," she said, leaving without giving Angela time to reply.

Angela settled back in her seat, feeling incredibly pleased with herself. She could feel the gaze of most of the cafeteria on her and the open-mouthed gapes of her friends were easily visible from the corner of her eye. The left side of her mouth twisted up into a smug, half-smile. Mitzi had come up to her, spoken to her, and most of all, had complimented something that she'd done. But wait. Angela suddenly came crashing back to reality. She hadn't done the things Mitzi thought she had. She hadn't sent those tweets! She suddenly remembered her plan to tell everyone that she didn't own the Twitter account, but that wouldn't work now. She had practically admitted to Mitzi that it was her account and couldn't go back on that.

Secretly, Angela found herself not caring. If her friends ditched her over this Twitter issue, she was fine with that because Mitzi liked what she was doing. Plus, if she kept doing what Mitzi liked, she might gain a coveted invitation into the popular group, which she really wanted.

Tessie snapped her out of her chain of thought. "So it is your Twitter account?" her voice was scathing and accusing.

Angela turned her head to Tessie, facing her head-on. She flipped her hair very slightly, just like Mitzi had done and then met Tessie's stare. She could have sworn that she saw the other girls' gaze flicker slightly, her confidence clearly decreasing. Angela twitched her head to the side slightly and said, "Yes, it is. Gotta Problem?"

"Yes!" Tessie exclaimed. "You can't send tweets that hurt people's feelings like that. That's just cruel."

"Freedom of speech," Angela said in reply. "I can write whatever I want. It says so in the law." She leaned forward, invading Tessie's personal space and causing the other girls' to shrink. "Deal...with...it." She grabbed her bag from where it was hanging over the back of her chair, stood up and walked out of the cafeteria. Tessie and the other girls watched her, their mouths agape.

Staring at her retreating figure, most of them realized that they didn't even recognize her anymore.

Diana sat alone at a table near the back of the cafeteria. She had watched the whole situation unfold and didn't know what to think. She had looked up the Twitter account on her iPad and had read the tweets. It had become clear that she had called it wrong as far as Angela was concerned. Angela was not the nice, friendly girl she had thought she was. Instead, she seemed cruel and shallow.

Chapter 6

Almost a week had passed since the incident in the cafeteria. The tweets continued to be sent - once, sometimes twice a day – and were always aimed at the weaker individuals in her year group. Angela had been gaining followers on the account incredibly fast; it seemed as if everyone in the school wanted to follow her. Of course, as her online popularity increased, so did her popularity in school. Everyone knew who she was, and whilst some people feared and many admired her, others now strongly disliked her.

Angela herself still had no idea who was actually running the account. She didn't tell anyone this though, not wanting to infringe upon her newfound popularity. For the entirety of her school life, she had been treated as if she was average and unpopular. Things had changed now and she didn't see the harm of allowing the Twitter account to keep running- it wasn't really hurting anyone.

She liked where she was at. Nearly everyone she passed would wave at her and everyone wanted to be her friend. She thought that people treated her like this because they generally liked her and her actions. She seemed to have forgotten the nasty nature of the tweets. People weren't trying to be her friend because they liked her. It was because they were terrified of her, and didn't want to be the subject of one of her internet jabs.

As for her old group of friends, certain girls such as Tessie, had opted to change tables in order to sit away from Angela. They disapproved of what she was doing and did not want to associate with her. However, these girls were the minority; the majority of girls were in awe of Angela. In their eyes, she had managed to pull herself out of social obscurity and made a name for herself. They weren't concerned with her methods - they just loved the fact that someone who was so similar to them was suddenly so well known. They wanted to be associated with her, hoping that one day, they would be recognized too.

However, Angela hadn't yet realized that she couldn't be one person on the internet and a different person in school. People expected her cyber profile to be the same as her real one and Angela understood this through one particular incident.

She was passing through the corridors with Kylie on her way to fourth-period English class, when she accidentally tripped a girl named Lacy. Lacy hit the floor hard and her papers were scattered all over the corridor. Angela felt guilty and tried to lean down to help pick up her things that were spread out all over the floor. However, she was prevented from doing so by Kylie, who seized her arm and hauled her away from the scene.

"What was that about?" Angela asked Kylie, somewhat irritated.

"Don't you get it?" Kylie was a little surprised, turning to look at the still confused Angela.

"No."

"Okay, look. You're being mean to try and move yourself up in the social hierarchy of high school, right? If you're doing this by making wonderful use of online tools, like Twitter, You HAVE to act in a similar manner as you do online, even IN school. Everyone knows who you are, and what you're like through this account of yours. They think they know you. If people see that you're acting differently in school, they'll think that you're a fake. "

"So, I have to be mean in school as well?"

"If you want to keep up this popularity, then yeah," Kylie gave Angela a knowing look before walking into English and taking her seat. Angela entered after her and sat down slowly, mulling over what Kylie had just told her. It was true, she knew. In person, she had to act like her virtual self. She had to become the person that someone else had created for her, in order to keep her social status. If she was found to be faking things, there was no doubt in her mind that instead of climbing up the social ladder, she'd be pushed down to the very bottom of the rung.

She had to change her behaviour. She had to start making rude, nasty comments about people during school and Angela knew that she could. After all, she had made rather malicious comments to Diana's face before. She just needed to expand her web, picking out other students who could be targets.

The lesson had started, but Angela couldn't be bothered with the themes in Of Mice and Men. She had much more important things to do. Pulling out her notebook, she looked around her class. She thought about people in her other classes who were quiet and mostly ignored. She wrote down every single name that popped into her head. These people were her new targets and Angela thought - smiling maliciously, there was one person who she knew she'd be able to confront with ease. The one person who couldn't fight back, simply because she was too scared to do so. Picking up her pen again, Angela drew a circle around the name. Diana.

Angela didn't want to waste any time in putting her little plan into action. There was a strong possibility that the rumors regarding her apparent "fakeness" had already begun to circulate and she wanted to dispel them as soon as possible. Therefore, she decided to start working from lunchtime - on that very same day. At that point, she didn't feel like targeting her main target, Diana. Instead, she would start with someone else on her list.

She walked across the field with a new sense of confidence. She could feel people's gazes fixed on her and could hear their whispers. She smiled to herself as she thought about how just a couple of weeks ago, nobody would bother about her. It was surprising what a few mean tweets sent from someone who was posing as her could do and sent that person a silent "Thank you". She didn't know why they had done it, but it had ended up making her life much better.

Walking into the cafeteria, she looked around, surveying the room. She spotted Tracy, one of the girls on her target list, paying for food at one of the cafeteria lines and zeroed in.

"Hi Tracy," Angela cooed as she approached the unsuspecting girl.

Tracy looked at Angela strangely. They had never spoken before and Tracy had heard about Angela's recent unfriendly behavior over the internet. She had no idea why Angela would be talking to her and was actually feeling slightly afraid. "Hi Angela," she said cowardly.

"What are you getting?" Angela continued to speak in a high-pitched voice, the kind of voice someone might use when speaking to a young child. It was rather intimidating and Tracy felt uncomfortable.

"Um, just the spaghetti," Tracy looked down at her paper plate. It was oozing with tomato sauce and little spaghetti worms. Angela looked down at it and made a disgusted face.

"Oh, I see. Trying to put on ten more kilograms before Christmas break?" Angela looked up and down Tracy. "Really, you should be trying to lose some of that baby fat. We're not in elementary anymore." She walked off, leaving poor Tracy standing there, with her jaw on the floor. Angela felt a little victorious. She looked around and noticed that several people had been observing the incident. News travels fast, she knew that by the end of the day, everybody would know about what had happened and she loved that. There was no way that she would be regarded as a fake now. She was ready.

Chapter 7

Another week went by, devoid of any significant events. Angela had continued to target the people listed in her notebook, using several different methods. She would directly confront them in a manner similar to what she did to Tracy and made snide comments whenever one of them spoke in class, or during breaks. She would laugh at them, poke fun at them and just generally be unfriendly.

The person who was tortured the most was Diana. Her fear of confrontation, accent and the fact that she had no friends to stick up for her, made her the easiest target. Angela made it a habit of delivering at least one rude comment to Diana's face every day. Rose often saw these and tried to comfort Diana afterwards.

This behavior was noticed by everyone else. Some approved of it, going by the theory of survival of the fittest. Others were not so admiring, however, they kept silent, not expressing their disapproval for fear that Angela would turn on them as well. Mitzi, naturally had noticed Angela's change in conduct and wholeheartedly supported it. She actually sspoke to Angela, often said hi in the corridors, or made small conversation. Angela loved this and was over the moon.

She was buying a sausage roll for her morning break when she heard someone approaching behind her. She turned around to see who it was; Kylie was standing there. "Hey," Angela greeted her with a smile as she handed her money over to the cashier, before moving out of the queue. "What's up?"

"Listen, I get why you're doing this whole 'evil Angela' thing. I mean, you want to be popular and who doesn't? But with this latest tweet of yours, you've gone too far. Before this, they were just little insults, no big deal, but you can't go around telling people that they don't deserve to be alive. That's just really mean."

Angela had no idea what Kylie was talking about. She'd never seen that tweet before and she had checked the Twitter account before she had left home in the morning. She did this to ensure that if any of the tweets that people thought had been sent by her came up, she'd know what people were talking about and be able to discuss them as if she had been the one who wrote them. But here she was, caught off guard. She wasn't prepared to tell Kylie that it wasn't actually her that had sent the tweet, as that would just blow her cover. So she acted as if she was perfectly aware of the subject of Kylie's speech. "Um, yeah! Yeah, I thought I might have gone too far with that one. Sorry. It won't happen again."

"It's not really me you should be apologizing to. You should apologize to Summer," Kylie said, before walking off, leaving Angela standing in the middle of the cafeteria.

Angela felt a wave of guilt wash through her. Summer was a nice girl whom she had known since Grade 6. Angela had gone to her for help with maths several times through the years and Summer had always been sweet and accommodating, taking time out of her schedule to help Angela with whatever problems she had. Although she was relatively unpopular and quiet, Angela had left her off her target list because of all of the assistance she had given her and she really liked her.

When Angela got home that day, she logged onto her computer. She had received several other comments regarding the tweet that Kylie had told her about. Some were approving, while others were disapproving. Mitzi had said that it was yet another stroke of evil genius and that Angela clearly knew how to "push people to their breaking point", something she deemed a "useful skill in today's tumultuous world". Angela felt that if Mitzi approved, it was alright, however, she found herself feeling very uneasy having not actually seen the tweet with her own eyes. She wanted to know what the person posing as her was saying.

She clicked on Safari and opened up the Twitter page. The tweet that everyone was talking about was at the top and it was in response to a tweet from Summer, that excitedly proclaimed that she'd gotten into the exclusive summer program of a top university in the country.

SummerR: Don't think that this makes you special or anything. You're still as worthless as ever. People like you don't deserve to be alive.

Angela felt her mouth drop open as she read the tweet. She re-read it and absorbed each pernicious word. She agreed wholeheartedly with what Kylie had said earlier;

this was taking it too far. She suddenly wished that she could take this whole thing back, wished that she could tell people the truth that this wasn't her Twitter account and never had been. Opening a new tab, she typed in Facebook's web address. Her homepage came up, and she was so very tempted to type a long post explaining the dilemma she was in to all of her Facebook friends. Explaining that the Twitter account wasn't hers, that someone was posing as her. But it wouldn't work. She'd openly admitted that the account was hers and nobody would believe her anymore.

She noticed that she had a message. She clicked on her inbox icon and saw that the unread letter was from Summer. It was one single sentence. Don't expect any help from me, ever again.

Angela looked down at her carpeted bedroom floor. She was ashamed of herself, for accepting that the account was hers when it wasn't. She should have seen this coming, seen that it would backfire on her. She didn't really want to hurt people. Of course she wanted to be popular, but she didn't want to make other people who had helped her feel as if they were worthless. She typed a reply to Summer's message,

"I'm so sorry".

Summer was obviously online, because she wrote back almost instantly. "If you're so sorry, delete the tweet".

Angela was stuck again. She couldn't delete the tweet, simply because the account wasn't hers. She couldn't even guess the password because she had no idea who was running the account. She had let someone else, someone unknown to her, take control of her life. She clicked back to the Twitter account and scrolled through it. It was unbelievable how this person seemed to know everything about her and was able to imitate her so well. It scared her to death, but there was nothing she could do. When she scrolled back up, she saw that there was a new tweet, in reply to a tweet about the entire Summer situation.

TessieSThomas: You're taking Summer's side? Fine. It makes my day a whole lot nicer not having to see your disgustingly ugly face.

Angela gasped and buried her head in her hands. Everything was so out of control. It had gone too far, but there was no way to put a stop to it. Angela felt as if she was trapped in a cell that had no doors, or windows. Only walls; and they were closing in on her. There was no way she could escape that horrible cell.

She thought it was bad then, but it was about to get even worse.

Chapter 8

The tweets were gradually getting more malevolent, and Angela was becoming more and more uneasy about the situation that she was in. However, she still had not told anyone that it was not her account, because she was too scared of what might happen to her if people discovered she had been lying to them all along. Looking back on the entire incident now, Angela wished that she had told someone. It would have helped her.

Thursday evening brought stormy weather; the wind was strong and raging, blowing with such force that the trees had to struggle to stay upright. The rain was heavy, flooding streets and making roads impossible to travel on. The thunder and lightning were menacing, filling everyone with a great amount of fear. Edmonton was like a ghost-town with each resident opting to stay in the comfort of their homes, rather than venture out. Angela too was sitting quietly at her desk, finishing off her History essay. She thought that perhaps the person behind the Twitter account wouldn't post any new tweets today, opting to give her a respite. Boy was she wrong.

Across town, the person impersonating Angela stared out of the window at the grey sky and smiled sinisterly. The storm was perfect! It was the kind of weather that managed to create the atmosphere needed to put the imposters' plans into action.

From the very beginning, the imposter had wanted to ruin Angela. The Twitter account had been created because this person was under the impression that by sending out mean tweets to people, Angela would seem undesirable and mean. Although some parts of the plan had worked perfectly, a majority of it had also backfired. Angela had gained notoriety and popularity from the account - a result that was neither planned nor wanted, but now, the imposter was about to put everything back on track and send Angela spiralling down the rabbit hole.

This person had been planning this for quite some time now, observing and figuring out who should be the target. The criteria for identifying the one who the message would be aimed at was simple; the target had to be someone who would react in an extreme manner. Therefore, the person had to be someone sensitive, someone who took things to heart. The target had been established.

Sitting down at a computer, the person logged into the Twitter account and began to type out a message.

Rosie831: I can't believe that you're still around. If I were you, I'd have killed myself by now. If you did, I bet nobody would even remember you.

Rose Evans had just turned on her laptop. She hated the stormy weather. In fact, ever since she was a little girl she had been terrified of storms and each time lightning flashed through the sky, illuminating it for a split second, she couldn't help but jump. She had drawn her curtains and decided to go online to try and distract herself from the gales blowing outside.

As the computer started up, Rose leaned back in her chair and sighed. She had a horrible day, but for her, every day was horrible. Not many people knew much about Rose, but each time she tried to interact with others, they either ignored her or called her mean names. This had been happening since she joined the middle school of San Christo High in grade six, after moving from Chicago. She'd begged her parents to move her out of the school and they had wanted to, but the only other institute in Edmonton was a private school, which they simply could not afford. So Rose went through each day and tried to keep her head up high. She didn't want anyone to see that she wasn't happy, especially her parents. They really did so much for her, and she didn't want to break their hearts.

Things had perked up for her at the beginning of eighth grade and she had finally made friends. A new girl joined San Christo High at that time and as with schools in most small towns, found herself alienated and uncomfortable among people who had known each other since kindergarten. Rose herself had been the last new girl to join and therefore felt sorry for the girl. She felt she could identify with the new girl and they became friends. The new girl was eventually accepted into another group of girls and she had brought Rose along with her. For once, Rose felt as if she belonged and they all seemed to like her a lot. They complimented her on the way she was always genuinely nice, the way she looked out and cared for others. They even called her the "mother hen", the first nice nickname that Rose had in a while

However, everything had changed at the beginning of this year, which was her freshman year. Over the summer, Rose had gone to visit her old friends and family back in Chicago and therefore had been absent from Edmonton. While she had been gone, her friends had a falling out and the group had dispersed. Upon returning a couple of days before school started, Rose had found that she was left without a group of friends and all her former friends had been absorbed into other groups. One had even joined Angela's circle. Rose however, was stuck all alone.

The teasing had resumed as school started and Rose found herself being targeted again, becoming the subject of many underhanded comments, which were generally about her weight or her looks. Rose was slightly overweight and had a tendency to have sudden breakouts of acne; both of these were things that she was rather self-conscious and insecure about. Rose was also the kind of person who took everything to heart. She was very sensitive and even the slightest unkind comment could make her feel horrible. This was the source of her weight; if there was a problem Rose would eat her feelings out of it.

Today, she had been coming out of swimming lessons at around four-thirty, a couple of hours before the storm had hit. Rose had taken up swimming as a sport to try and lose weight, because she was useless at any of the other games. Team sports had always treated her badly, as she was often forced to sit on the sidelines. As she closed the gate to the swim area, she was confronted by several girls and instantly recognized a few of her former friends in the group.

"Um, hi guys," she had said, nervously.

They had ignored her greeting and started in on the insults almost immediately. They had teased her about trying to lose weight, telling her quite frankly that it wasn't working and told her she had no friends. They told her that she was alone, she had no one to stand up for her and that nobody liked her. Rose just stood there while they spoke and tried not to cry. The insults kept hitting her and piercing her skin like bullets. The minute that they paused to gather up more ammunition, she ran and she didn't stop until she got home.

The more she thought about it now, the more she realized that they were actually correct in everything they said. She didn't have friends and she did seem to repel people slightly. Rose had tried so hard to befriend Diana, who she again identified with because of the teasing. However, Diana always pushed her away and Rose didn't understand why; it wasn't as if Diana had any friends herself. If she was in her shoes, she would welcome the gesture, glad that someone in this unfriendly town was willing to make her feel comfortable and happy.

There must be something wrong with me, Rose thought to herself as she opened up her internet browser. There must be a reason why people don't like me and always seem to push me away. It must be my fault. I mean, if someone else tries to be friendly towards another person, they'll welcome it. If I try, they'll just push me away. Am I worthless? Am I beneath people?

She opened up her Twitter account, typed in her password and as her dashboard opened, she noticed that she had a mention. Excitement flashed through her; Rose hardly ever got mentions, not having any friends to talk to on Twitter and few followers who actually cared about her tweets. The mention appeared on her screen and she read it slowly. As each word registered in her mind, she felt her excitement dwindle and her spirits sank. She blinked and then read the sentence again.

The minute that she had seen it was from Angela's Twitter handle, her excitement had turned into fear. Although she didn't have friends, she still heard the rumors and stories that circulated around school. The topic of interest that had been making the rounds recently was about Angela, and how she was sending despicable messages to people over Twitter. Although she had been gaining notoriety for it, Rose resented what she had been doing. How could someone become popular for sending out messages that hurt other people's feelings? She had read the tweets and had thought about how much she would hate for one of those tweets to be directed towards her; but she knew that the day would come. Angela was targeting those people in their grade who didn't have that many friends, who weren't as popular and those who had some feature about them that made them easy to tease or target. Rose knew she was one of them. Angela had already made a couple of mean comments to her in school and Rose knew that a tweet would be coming her way.

Reading this tweet that had been sent to her, it seemed as if Angela had been saving the worst for her. Her tweets had started off as tiny insults that people who were even the slightest bit tougher than Rose would be able to handle without breaking a sweat. However, the tweets had gradually built up, became more hurtful and now, they had turned into something completely despicable. Rose couldn't quite believe what she was reading.

Slowly it started to sink in and the words jumped out at her from the computer screen, suddenly appearing in front of her in 3D. Everything went blurry and the only thing that was clear was the insult that she had just received. Pain shot through her body and she felt as if she wanted to scream.

Lightning flashed outside, and she became even more tense. It was true, nobody liked her or wanted her around, a meaningless figure and someone who should never have existed. Even erasing her existence now would mean nothing to anybody. No one would care. They would light a candle for her, feature her on a Yearbook page to be polite, but that was it. No one would cry, no one would miss seeing her in the school halls and no one would even notice the difference.

Rose stumbled down the stairs, her face streaming with tears. Her parents weren't home, because they had gone to visit their lawyers and were likely to be stuck in the storm. She staggered into the kitchen and opened the first drawer of the cabinet. Fumbling around, she found a keychain containing several keys. She crossed the room, almost slipping on a tile that was wet from a freshly-sprung leak in the ceiling, to the wall where the medicine cabinet was located. She unlocked the cabinet and grabbed a bottle of Tylenol and slammed it onto the counter. Before she opened it, Rose took a pen from the holder and a post-it note from the stack that her mother used to write her shopping lists on. She scrawled out a note explaining what had been happening to her, the tweet from Angela, and how that had pushed her over the edge and made her realize that she couldn't and didn't want to deal with it anymore. She signed the note with one final sentence: "I'm sorry."

Then she uncapped the bottle and swallowed the pills.

Chapter 9

Rose wasn't in school the next day. Instead, she was in the hospital.

Her parents had reached home minutes after Rose had taken the pills. Luckily, they had arrived at the lawyer's office only to be told that their lawyer was not in, due to the fact that the storm had hit much earlier on his side of town and he didn't make it back to the office. The secretary told them that she had tried to contact them, but kept getting their voice mail service. Rose's parents had immediately started for home and had been stuck in the storm for an hour, but they got there at just the right time.

They came into the kitchen and saw their daughter lying on the ground, pills spilt all over the marble floor. Her mother gave out a bellowing scream, which even with the thunders and wind, the neighbours must have heard. She ran to the door shouting, "call 911, call 911". Traumatic as it must have been, Rose's father managed to keep a straight head, rushed over to her and immediately checked her pulse. At first, he couldn't find one, so he opened her mouth with his left hand forced his fore and middle finger down her throat. She gasped and when he didn't remove his fingers, vomit came flooding down his arm. Thankfully, the hospital was near their house and with the phone lines down in the storm, he raced to his car with his daughter cradled in his arm and drove like a madman through the storm. During the entire journey, her mother begged in the backseat, with Rose's head on her lap, tears streaming down her face; begged God to save her child. Pulling up to the hospital, her father jumped out of the front seat picked up his daughter and rushed into the A&E.

"She took all of them, all of them," her mother said as though all the strength had left her body.

All this time her father had not said a word; and as he had somewhat robotically taken charge of everything else, he leads his wife to the waiting area as she wailed. After almost an hour; the hardest hour of their lives, the doctor came out of the room where Rose was being treated to tell them that everything was going to be alright - that their daughter was going to pull through.

They saw Rose lying on the white hospital bed, with all sorts of wires and tubes hooked up to her. The doctor told them that she would need to stay there for a few more days, so that they could monitor her and make sure that all of the toxins were gone from her body or at least down to amounts which her body would be able to sustain. He told them that although she would be discharged within days, she would need to see a therapist at least weekly for quite some time. He eventually asked them the question that they knew was coming, but didn't want to think about: "do you have any idea why your daughter would try to kill herself?" It was then that Rose's mother remembered the crumpled up piece of paper that she was clutching in her right hand and with trembling fingers, she opened it up. As she skimmed through the contents of the letter, she held her belly and cried. At this time the doctor looked on, both worried and sympathetic.

Mrs. Evans started shaking and slowly stated, "someone told my child to kill herself." Her voice dull, body shaking as though a cold air had suddenly entered the waiting room; Rose's mother began to gaze at nothing.

"Mrs. Evans, I think we should give you something to calm down," the doctor offered.

As if to bring herself back to life, she shook her shoulders pulled her hair back with both hands, wiped her eyes and replied, "there's no need, my daughter needs me. I'm okay now."

Rose woke up the next morning, around ten o'clock and didn't know where she was at that moment. She looked around and all she could see was white. There were flowers by her bedside - Carnations, which her mother had run out to buy that morning. She tried to sit up and managed to do so, but with great pain. It was at that time that she looked down and saw that her leg was in a cast. She was hooked up to machines, wires protruding everywhere, but Rose didn't understand what had happened - she was confused and most of all, she was scared. Suddenly, the sound of the door opening caused her to look up.

Mr. and Mrs. Evans entered quietly. They didn't seem to realize that Rose was awake and therefore moved almost silently.

"Mom? Dad?" Rose asked, causing them to jump.

"Oh, Sweetie! You're up!" Mrs. Evans automatically pressed a blue button on the wall.

"Where am I? What...what happened?" Rose frowned, trying to figure out why she was in...the hospital?

Mrs. Evans sat down on the side of Rose's bed, being mindful of the various tubes and wires that were keeping tabs on Rose's vital signs, and giving her liquids to stabilize her. "You're in the hospital, honey. You...you swallowed some pills last night and..." Mrs. Evans trailed off. She didn't know what to say. What do you say to someone who's just tried to kill themselves and has been unsuccessful? How do you explain what has happened to them, when you barely understand it yourself?

However, even with that tiny prompt, Rose felt it all rushing back: the confrontation after her swimming lessons, the tweet from Angela, the haziness, the pain, the feeling of being worthless...it all flooded through her mind and overwhelming her. She remembered how conscious she was of the pills going down her throat, each one going down, down, down. She remembered the agony that had ripped her insides apart and remembered falling in slow motion through the air, until she hit the kitchen floor. And then...blackness.

"I remember," she said quietly. "But how did I get here? I'm not...dead."

"We came home in time. Your father saved you." Rose had begun to cry, and Mr. Evans reached forward and took her hand, entwining their fingers together.

"Oh my Rose, you could offer me all the flowers in the world but I'd only want my Rose. Nothing in the worl....." as he tried to sing his little song he's been singing to Rose since they named her in her mother's belly, tears started streaming down his face. He leaned over, pressing his lips against her forehead. "I couldn't live in this world without my precious Rose." He missed a few words, but in that moment he wanted her to know the most important thing in that song, he couldn't imagine life without her.

All three of them were crying now.

Mucus running down her nose, her cheeks and neck completely saturated with tears, she finally said, "nobody likes me, Dad. Nobody."

She slowly told her parents the entire story of what had happened. She told them everything, about how she felt as if she was worthless, as if no one cared about her and no one wanted her. She told them about how the tweet she had received made her feel that maybe she really shouldn't exist and told them the exact wording of the tweet. Her mother cried and with the pain his daughter must have felt now running through him, her father clenched his right fist kneading it into his left palm.

"What's that girls' full name?" Mrs. Evans asked?

"Angela Hernandez," Rose sniffed.

"Hernandez?!" she exclaimed. "Clara Hernandez's daughter? As in the family that lives in the old house down Cherison Lane?" Rose nodded. "Those people think that just because they have so much money they can do whatever they want, say whatever they want, hurt whomever they want. I've heard things about that Angela girl. A couple of other mothers down at school were saying that she's been sending some nasty messages around to other girls as well and saying some mean things. Well, that girl has bitten off more than she can chew! Her parents and their money won't be able to protect her now. I'm taking this straight to the police. Straight to the police!"

"No, Mom!" Rose felt as if her mother was over-reacting. Of course what Angela had done was serious, but did it warrant such an extreme reaction. "You don't need to do that, really! I mean... trying to kill myself was my choice and not Angela's. Plus, I'm sure the police department has more important things to deal with."

"Nonsense!" Mrs. Evans exclaimed. "What that girl has been doing has a name - cyber-bullying, and that is a crime! This case is extreme enough for her to be charged with a misdemeanor of cyber harassment and she will be! I'm not going to the school about this one, only to have them sit back and do nothing just as they did when you were being teased when you joined. Yes, your father and I did go to the principal, and all they said was that 'it's a stage she's going through, it'll end soon'. Well, this has gone too far! I am going STRAIGHT to the police whose job it is to protect EVERYONE! They will get justice for you Rose and all the other girls this little viper is attacking. I'll make sure that girl is punished for this and nothing will save her from my wrath. Nothing."

"I agree," Mr. Evans said, siding with his wife. "Richard and Clara Hernandez might be big-shots here in Edmonton, but that doesn't mean that their daughter can do something like this to someone else and get away unscathed. It won't happen. Not while I'm around. I promise you that I'll make sure that she is punished and can't hurt you...or anybody else, for that matter, again. After we've done that, we'll move. I don't care about my job, we'll find a new one back in Chicago, where you have friends and will be surrounded by people who love you. I'm sorry I got us into this. But I'll fix it."

Rose looked at her parents and laughed suddenly. Mrs. Evans looked at her in shock. "It isn't funny."

"I know," Rose said. "I'm just thinking about the fact that before I...you know, I thought that nobody cared about me. I'd forgotten that I have two people in my life who love me and care more than anyone else in the world." She reached forward as far as the many tubes and wires connected to her would allow and took her mothers' hand. "Both of you. Dad, you're willing to give up your job and move back to Chicago for me just so that I can be surrounded by my friends and be happy. Mom, you're ready to storm down to the police station and demand that the daughter of one of the most powerful people in town pays for what she's done to me. I was upset because I didn't have anyone who bothered enough about me to stand up for me, but I completely forgot that both of you are willing to go out there and fight for me." She smiled. "Thank you, Mom and Dad. I'm so glad that I didn't succeed because I know that I would have killed you too.

I didn't think it through and I promise to never do anything like that again."

"We love you too, Sweetie," Mrs. Evans squeezed her daughter's hand. "We will always protect you and fight for you. We are all in this together, so it's important that you are open and honest with us about everything and especially things like this."

Meanwhile, at San Christo High, Angela was strolling through the halls on her way to English class. She had seen the tweet that had been sent out to Rose last night, and she couldn't believe that she had let everything come this far. That tweet was despicable; something that she would never, ever say to another person. However, everyone thought that she had said it, and there was nothing she could do about it.

She was worried too, because Rose wasn't in school today and Angela feared that it had something to do with the tweet. She imagined how she must have felt reading it and couldn't fathom how she could have not been affected by it. She tried to think of how she would have felt if someone had said that to her and it made her cringe. She had wanted to find out what was up with Rose, but as Rose had no friends, she had no one whom she could ask. At break time, Angela had actually called up Rose's house, but there had been no answer.

She couldn't help but be scared.

Chapter 10

As it was the case in all other small towns, news in Edmonton travelled fast. Within an hour, it could traverse the entire town and you could bet that each and every resident would be talking about it...at least until the next juicy tidbit came along. However, this Saturday, the story wasn't the usual Mrs. Smith's dog ate Mrs. Jones's petunias or it turns out that there's a family of mice living in the changing rooms at the public pool. It was much more serious. Word had gotten out about Rose.

Angela had found out while doing her homework up in her room and she had gotten a call from Kylie.

"Hello?" she said, touching the green 'talk' button on the mobile's screen and bringing it up to her ear.

"I hope you're happy!" Kylie exclaimed angrily from the other end.

Angela was confused, but figured that it must have something to do with the Twitter account. Maybe the person had sent a message to Kylie. "What?" she asked.

"Oh, don't tell me you don't know!"

"I actually don't..." Angela said.

"That tweet you sent to Rose? You should have known better Angela! I mean, Jill's told us how sensitive she is and your comment was so...so evil that OF COURSE she took it to heart. It sent her barrelling over the edge. I mean, I would have probably done the same and I'm not even half as sensitive as her."

"Wait..." Angela wasn't sure what she was hearing. "What did Rose do?"

"Tried to kill herself! Swallowed a bunch of pills. Because of you!"

"Oh my God!" Angela suddenly felt dizzy. Nausea built up. She could feel acids tingling in her stomach and rising up through her oesophagus, until she could feel their fiery burn at the back of her throat. She couldn't see straight, everything was blurry, and everything was moving. She wanted to throw up. "Is...is she okay?"

"Thankfully, yes. Her parents found her in time. She's still in hospital though. I hope you're happy Angela. I'm so disgusted right now. I don't understand how you could do something like this, how you could not think of how something like that could have affected someone. You were such a nice person Angela, you always had been. I can't believe you. I don't even want to talk to you anymore. I don't want to be associated with you. Don't call me. Don't talk to me at school. Just forget we were ever friends." She cut the phone, and Angela was left listening to nothing.

How could something like this happen? How could the tame little Twitter account that she wasn't running get so out of hand? How could someone try to kill herself because of a tweet? Worst of all, everyone would think Angela had sent that tweet, because not only did the account bear her name, but she had told people that it was her account. She buried her face in her hands and felt her palms become damp with tears. She couldn't believe it. Rose had tried to kill herself over a tweet that she had allegedly sent. Nobody would believe that Angela hadn't sent it. They would think that she was a murderer!

She managed to get up from her chair and walk into her parents' room. They were both sitting at their computers, typing. "Mom...dad.." she said quietly, to get their attention.

"Angela honey, we're a bit busy," Mrs. Hernandez didn't even turn around to look at her daughter.

"Mom...you have to listen to me," she said it this time with more urgency, and her voice carried. This made her parents swivel around to face her, looking at her with bewildered expressions on their faces. Angela guessed that they hadn't heard yet, but she would rather that she told them, than they heard it from some angry, screaming person who deemed their daughter a murderer. She'd be able to tell them the true story, what was really happening and how she wasn't behind the Twitter account at all. They would understand or rather, they should understand.

"I have something to tell you..." she began. However, she couldn't finish telling them what she wanted to. The doorbell rang.

Chapter 11

Angela Hernandez had lived in Edmonton for her whole life. In the many years she had spent in the town, she had been everywhere: the main shopping street, the central fountains and the historical statue of the first settler in Edmonton. She had skipped class by hiding in the bushes at the back of San Christo High, explored the woods in the East of the town and had strolled down Main Street savoring a huge ice-cream sundae from Edmonton's renowned and only ice cream parlour. However, never had she sat in the police station.

Mrs. Evans had acted on her word and had gone to the police, who told her that they would bring Angela in for questioning. It turned out that cyber-bullying was indeed taken very seriously in their town and could result in a felony charge.

Angela had opened the door to find a policeman standing outside. He requested to see her parents and informed them that Angela needed to be taken in for questioning over an alleged case of cyber-bullying, that almost resulted in the death of another girl. This was the first time that Angela's parents had heard anything of the sort and looked rather confused. However, they accompanied their daughter to the police station, sure that nothing would come of the visit as Angela was clearly not guilty of anything. Angela was silent. She knew that she was guilty. She might not have been behind the Twitter account, she might not have sent the tweet, but she hadn't done anything to let anyone know that the account wasn't hers. Now, she was about to face the consequences.

She was taken to a room by one of the police detectives, where both parents and her were seated on uncomfortable chairs which faced a desk. The lighting was harsh and the air conditioning was on full blast, making Angela wish that she'd brought a jacket along.

The door behind them opened and Angela turned around. A tall man, with dark brown hair and weathered skin entered. He wasn't wearing a police uniform, but he had a badge hanging around his neck at the end of a thin, silver chain. There was a name-tag pinned onto the breast pocket of his leather jacket. Angela squinted to try and read it, but she couldn't. He closed the door and walked over to the desk. Placing the files he was holding on the desk, he pulled out the chair and sat down. "Mr. and Mrs. Hernandez, Angela, I'm Detective Stevens."

"Hello Detective," Mr. Hernandez reached out and shook the man's hand. "We were told that you wanted to see Angela regarding a cyber-bullying case?"

"That's correct," Detective Stevens replied shortly. He didn't offer any further explanation. Angela guessed that he wanted to see how much her parents knew about the situation, before he provided any details. She shifted uncomfortably in her chair.

"Well," Mr. Hernandez continued, trying to appear unfazed. "We believe that you're mistaken. Angela is a very kind girl, and would never bully anyone. You must have mixed her up with someone else. We can vouch that she hasn't done anything of the sort."

"Are you sure?" Detective Stevens' question caught Mr. Hernandez off-guard.

"Am I sure? Yes, of course I am sure! I know my daughter!"

"Modern studies have shown that nowadays, parents think that they know their children, when in reality, they know very little about them. I believe that this is the case with you and Angela, Mr. Hernandez."

"Look, I'm not here to get psychoanalyzed about my relationship with my daughter," Mr. Hernandez was clearly quite angry. "Now, I have a lot of work to do and I'm fully aware that I can just take my family and walk out of here. So, unless you have some relevant questions to ask us, that is exactly what I will do. I'm not about to waste my time."

"I apologize. We'll get straight to the point, shall we? Mr. and Mrs. Hernandez, are you familiar with a girl named Rose Evans?"

"I don't know majority of the children in this town, except for my daughter's close friends," Mr. Hernandez replied. "My wife might though," he turned to Mrs. Hernandez, who had a thoughtful expression on her face.

"Rose Evans..." she mumbled. "Ah yes! The blonde girl. Daughter of that couple that moved here from Chicago a few years ago, I believe. Brenda! Yes, that's her name and her daughter is Rose, right?" Mrs. Hernandez faintly remembered welcoming Brenda, Rose's mother, to the neighborhood several years ago, and finding out that she had a daughter of the same age as Angela named Rose. Mrs. Hernandez hadn't spoken to Brenda for a long time, and therefore her memory was slightly hazy. However, Detective Stevens nodded in approval.

"That's correct. Angela, do you know Rose?"

Angela nodded. "I do," she said quietly. "She's in my grade at school."

"Do you talk to her?"

"Not really."

"Have you ever spoken to her?"

"I think once, for a project." Angela had actually spoken to her several other times over recent days. She had made a couple of derogatory comments about Rose's weight to her face, but they had been tiny little things, nothing worth getting this upset over.

"Does she have many friends?"

"I don't know. I don't think so. I never really see her with anyone. I think she sits alone," Angela tried to remember seeing Rose in school, but it was hard, considering that she never really noticed Rose that much. "She used to hang around with a bunch of girls last year. I don't really remember who exactly, but I think that they had a fight or something because the entire group split up."

"Excuse me, Detective," Mr. Hernandez interrupted. "My daughter has made it clear that she doesn't know this Rose girl very well. What is the relevance of these questions? What does this girl have to do with my daughter?"

"I take it you are unaware of what happened to Rose Evans two nights ago?"

"I do not keep up with the gossip of this town." Mr. Hernandez turned to his wife, "Darling, do you know anything?"

Mrs. Hernandez shook her head. "I'm afraid I don't."

"Two nights ago, Rose Evans received a particularly malicious message over the social networking site,

Twitter. She was so distraught over it, that she tried to kill herself. She overdosed on Tylenol."

Mrs. Hernandez brought her hand to heart, visibly shocked. "Oh, that's terrible! The poor family. I must send over flowers at once. White lilies, I think and we must attend the funeral. I'll have to buy a new black suit. We must all....."

Detective Stevens brought his hand up and Mrs. Hernandez stopped speaking. "Rose did not succeed in killing herself. Her parents found her before it was too late and took her to the hospital, where they pumped her stomach. She is well on her way to making a full recovery."

"Detective, our deepest sympathies are with this girl and her family," her father interrupted yet again. "But what does this have to do with our daughter? What does it have to do with Angela?"

"Mr. Hernandez, you may recall my mentioning that Rose received a tweet before she attempted to commit suicide. This tweet was sent from your daughter's Twitter handle."

"What?" Mr. Hernandez turned to face Angela, who looked down. "Angela, tell me this isn't true."

"Mr. Hernandez, Mrs. Hernandez, were you aware that Angela had a Twitter account?"

"No, we weren't," Mrs. Hernandez admitted. "But we believe that our daughter should have freedom on the Internet. We allow her to do what she wants, and since she is over the age of thirteen, she is legally eligible to sign up for accounts on numerous sites without our permission anyway."

"We accessed Angela's page and read through some of the tweets. It appears that Rose isn't the only person that she's been targeting; she's targeted various students in her year by sending them mean message and this has been occurring for around two weeks. Such messages constitute as cyber-bullying, which is taken very seriously here in Edmonton." He paused and turned to his computer, where he typed in a couple of commands. He moved the desktop screen around so that it was visible to the Hernandez's. "I'd like you to read some of these."

Mr. and Mrs. Hernandez leaned forward to read the tweets. They couldn't believe what they were reading and didn't feel that the things written on the screen were things that their daughter would have said. Detective Stevens turned the screen around again and settled back in his chair. He didn't say anything, allowing them time to process what they had just seen.

"I think Angela should be allowed a chance to explain," Mr. Hernandez finally said. "Those tweets aren't things that she would send."

Detective Stevens looked Angela in the eye. For the first time, Angela understood what it was like to be pushed into a corner, to be intimidated. His gaze was steely and made Angela feel like she was insignificant, like she didn't matter. She couldn't believe that she had made other people feel like that. That wasn't her. She couldn't believe that she had let the person running the Twitter account take over her life like this. "Angela?"

She had to tell the truth now. "It's not my account," she said, quietly. "I didn't write all of those things. I know that they have my name on them, and the account seems like it's mine because it sounds like me, and the description sounds like something I would write about myself, but it isn't mine. I don't know how whoever created this account got all the information about me, but they did and now everyone thinks this account is mine, but it isn't, I swear. I would never say something like that to anyone."

"Alright," Detective Stevens had written everything down. "Well, we have no further questions at this point in time. Thank you, Mr. and Mrs. Hernandez. Angela. You are free to go."

"Excuse me Detective, but I have a question," Mr. Hernandez spoke up again. "If Angela is found guilty of cyber-bullying, which I'm certain she won't be as she has already made it clear to you that she is not the one behind this account, what would be the result?"

"Well, it would go on her permanent record for sure. She could be charged with a misdemeanor of cyber-harassment, which, as she is a minor, would result in her having to serve community service time. However, you will find that her main problem will arise when she has to apply to colleges. They prefer spotless records and may find that a history of cyber-bullying will have a negative influence. After all, nowadays cyber-bullying is taken very seriously."

Mr. Hernandez took a few moments to process this and Angela was standing there, in shock. She couldn't believe that a Twitter account that was originally giving her popularity, was amounting to so much trouble. It was literally ruining her life and suddenly, she didn't care about popularity. She wished she hadn't cared so much two weeks ago, when she could have actually changed something. She could have told people it wasn't her account and as a result, would have had a solid defense now. But, it was far too late for that.

She got into the back seat of her parent's car and before starting the vehicle up, Mr. Hernandez turned around to face her. "Angela, I want you to explain everything to us. Now."

Chapter 12

Angela was called back down to the police station on Sunday and her parents accompanied her again. She was sitting back in the same office, with the same painfully bright lights and blasting air conditioning. This time, however, she'd remembered to bring a jacket.

Detective Stevens entered the room, but this time, he was with someone else. It was another man and clearly a lot younger than Detective Stevens. He wasn't in uniform and wore a badge similar to that of the older detective, so Angela guessed that he was a rookie who had recently been promoted. Detective Stevens was probably showing him the ropes.

"Mr. and Mrs. Hernandez, Angela," Detective Stevens nodded. "Good to see you again. This is Detective Carson Randall," he motioned to the man next to him. "He'll be assisting me on the case."

"So this is a full-fledged case now?" Mr. Hernandez asked.

"Please understand that Edmonton is a small town," Detective Stevens smiled. "Nearly everything here becomes a case, be it a murder – which thankfully has yet to occur and hopefully never will – or who put the neighbors' cat up the tree. We're just trying to figure out exactly what has happened here so that Angela doesn't get blamed for something that she didn't do."

"Oh, so you've decided that Angela isn't to be blamed and that she wasn't behind the Twitter account?" Mrs. Hernandez perked up.

"Not quite," Detective Stevens answered. "We're still open to the option that she wasn't responsible. However, the evidence points to the fact that she was indeed behind the account."

"Evidence? What evidence?"

"We interviewed a few students from the school yesterday, after you had left," Detective Stevens held his hand out and Detective Randall handed him a file. He flicked it open and turned to the appropriate page. " Summer Randolph, Tessie Gradenheart and Mitzi Simmons. They all said that you have publicly declared that the account was yours. Tessie did say that you expressed some uncertainty when she first confronted you about the account, however, you confirmed that you were indeed behind it the very next day when she asked you directly. Summer Randolph said that she heard you boasting about the account to Mitzi Simmons, who confirmed that this was true. She also said that you seemed rather proud of the messages that you were sending to people. Now, this all contradicts what you told us yesterday; that you weren't actually behind the account and that someone else is running it. Why would you tell everyone else that you were running the account if it wasn't true? They also told me that you were being relatively mean in school as well, recently. They said that you were targeting all of the weaker kids in school."

"Angela," Mrs. Hernandez said quietly. "I think you'd better tell the detectives here everything."

"That would be nice," Detective Stevens supplemented.

"Okay, look," Angela turned back to the detectives. "Two weeks ago, Tessie confronted me at break or maybe it was lunch. I don't remember, but it doesn't really matter.

She accused me of sending a mean tweet to a girl in our grade. I had no idea what she was talking about. I didn't have a Twitter account and had no intention of getting one. I told her that she must be mistaken, that she must have read the name of the sender wrong. She was sure she hadn't. I asked her to send me the link to the page. She didn't see the need as she thought it was my account, but agreed anyway. So she sent me the link over Facebook. I saw the account, and I read the tweets that had been sent at the time. I didn't like them- they weren't things that I would say and I decided that the next day I would tell everyone that the account wasn't mine."

"So why didn't you?" Detective Stevens asked.

"Please, let me finish. So....... I was fully prepared to tell everyone the truth. At break-time, I sat down at the table and Tessie asked me if I'd seen the account. I told her I had and I was just about to tell her that it wasn't mine and that someone was posing as me, when Mitzi walked up. Yes, the same Mitzi that you interviewed. She's also the most popular girl at school. For years I have wanted to be just like her and be in her circle, but she's barely ever said a word to me. Anyway, she came over and complimented me on a mean tweet that she thought I had sent. She said it was genius and I was so stunned, but happy that she was talking to me, I confirmed that the account was mine. I decided that it didn't matter if it wasn't really my account - especially if I was going to become popular from it."

"And did you?"

"I kind of did. People started to talk to me more, smile at me in corridors, waved at me and everyone knew who I was. I think...maybe it was because they were scared that they would become the subject of one of my jabs on Twitter. But I still liked it. I didn't think of telling anyone that the tweets weren't being sent by me. Later, my friend Kylie told me that if I was going to be mean on the internet, I had to be mean in person. That's why I started making mean comments to people even in school. I'd already been fairly rude to Diana in the past, and she was an easy target, what with being the new girl she wouldn't want to retaliate, which is why she was the one I was the meanest to. Anyway, the tweets started to get nastier and made me uncomfortable, but I didn't see what I could do and then this happened."

Angela looked up. "I'm sorry I didn't tell anyone, but I didn't send those tweets. It's someone else, who's pretending to be me. What's it called when that happens?"

"Are you insinuating that you're a victim of identity theft?"

"Yes!" Angela exclaimed. "Yes, that's exactly what's happened! Someone stole my identity!"

Detective Stevens nodded. "Okay, then. We'll keep that in mind. Thank you for coming down."

After Angela and her parents had left, Detective Stevens turned to Detective Randall. "Well, Randall, you're the young one here. What do you think? Angela's story seem plausible to you?"

"I think she might be telling the truth, sir. After all, popularity means a lot to kids these days. I don't know how it was in your time, but it was everything when I was in college so I can imagine how much worse it's gotten. The media glamourises it. She might have done all of this just for popularity, but the question is, if someone did steal her identity, who did, and why?"

"That's always the question, isn't it? Okay, well, we'll have to look into this. It's not like we have anything else to do."

"True."

Chapter 13

Angela did not want to go to school on Monday. In fact, she was dreading it. She knew that everyone would know about Rose, about there being an ongoing police investigation into her. She'd already been receiving hate phone calls from other students, angry parents, siblings and even a couple of grandparents. It had gotten so bad that she had turned off her cell phone and her parents had disconnected their landline.

She had tried to convince her parents to let her stay at home, but they insisted that she continued to go to school. It wasn't a punishment; they believed her story completely, but they didn't want her to miss out on any learning. The chances of this incident being imprinted onto Angela's permanent record were high and her parents felt that she needed to work as hard as she could so that when it came time for college, they would look past the looming black mark.

She went to school and trudged through the hallways, silently. No one accompanied her - instead, everyone stuck to the sides, whispering and accusing her;

'That's Angela Hernandez, the girl who sents out all those mean tweets.'

'Yeah, she's in so much trouble now.'

'Oh, that's Angela, the one who sent that message to Rose?'

'You know the one that made her try to kill herself?'

'Angela Hernandez must be ashamed of herself.'

'I saw the police outside her house yesterday. Apparently, she's going to get charged with cyber-harassment. It's going to go on her permanent record. If you ask me, it serves her right. Rose did nothing to hurt her, so why should she hurt Rose?'

Angela sat alone at both lunch and break, because none of her old friends wanted to be associated with her. As far as they were concerned, the Angela Hernandez that they knew had disappeared, to be replaced with someone they didn't recognize. Instead, several of the girls who Angela had been mean to either in person or over Twitter had been welcomed into their group. They all sat together, laughing and finally understanding what it was like to belong. Even Diana had been welcomed and had accepted the invitation. She felt horrible about what had happened to Rose. If perhaps she had spoken to Rose and became her friend, she wouldn't have acted so rashly. As for Angela, Diana believed that she had gotten what was coming to her and she deserved to be an outcast. Now she knew what it felt like. Diana openly voiced her opinion on Angela, but kept her opinion on Rose strictly to herself.

Angela had been targeted through the day. Several people had had things to say to her and none of them were nice. They called her names and made her feel horrible. No one felt guilty about this, because they all just wanted Angela to feel like the people she had bullied. They had all decided that she would get what was coming to her and as such, everyone had turned against her.

The person running the account watched all of this from the outside and felt victorious. The imposter had finally brought Angela down, but something didn't feel quite right. Something felt incomplete and more had to be done. The imposter felt that eventually, Angela would recover from this and that eventually people would begin to accept her again. Something had to happen that would make sure that Angela didn't ever regain anyone's trust. This person had so much power over Angela's life that with a snap of a finger, things could change, but what action would help the imposter achieve the outcome that would ruin Angela's reputation for good.

Upon returning home the imposter opened the laptop and scrolled through Angela's Facebook page. What a laugh! Angela still hadn't realized how easy it was to impersonate her. She probably didn't even know that all of her information on Facebook was open - too bad for her. The imposter continued to scroll, looking for something that could be used against Angela. BINGO! There it was staring right up in the face.

It was a post from two weeks ago. It was a webcam picture of a credit card, along with the caption "I get to use my parents' credit card whenever I want! Thank you SO much Mom & Dad!" Angela probably hadn't realized at the time of posting what damage could be done with this photo. After saving the photo on the desktop, the imposter then opened it up in Photoshop.

The picture was fairly clear to start off with. The lighting was right, and the quality was good. Angela clearly had a steady hand, because the picture was barely blurred. Still, the person ran the picture through several sharpening filters, to save time and make sure that no mistakes were made. This was a risky job, much riskier than setting up a Twitter account and sending messages to people in Angela's grade.

Upon zooming in, the imposter was delighted that each number on the card was visible and easily readable. This was a tiny instrument that could do a lot of damage and make sure that Angela was never trusted again. Not even by her own parents.

Chapter 14

Angela told her parents about the horrible week she had at school on Sunday. Her parents finally decided that it would be best if she stayed at home for a day, hoping that the whole thing would blow over. However, they made her promise that she would email her teachers asking about the work that she had missed, so that she could catch up.

She was walking downstairs at about ten in the morning to fix herself a snack, when she saw her mother standing by the door, looking rather puzzled. She was holding a sheet of paper in her hands, reading intently.

"Mom?" Angela asked, approaching her. Mrs. Hernandez looked up. "What's happened? Is it something to do with the case?" Angela was scared that there had been some new development that would incriminate her. She didn't want this to go on her permanent record and would rather just forget all about it.

"The Case? No, it's nothing to do with the case. It's something else."

"What?" Angela was confused.

"We received our credit card bill and it's huge. We didn't even order a majority of the things on this list. Like what use would we have for a packet of 350 copic markers? I don't even know what copic markers are!"

"Relax, mom," Angela tried to act reassuring. "I'm sure the credit card company made a mistake. Maybe they got it all mixed up and sent you the wrong bill."

"I hope so, because I am certainly not paying for all of these things," Mrs. Hernandez exclaimed. "Your father is not going to be happy. He's already stressed out, as it is with this cyber-bullying thing against you. Angela, you didn't do it, right? You didn't bully Rose, you didn't send out any of those tweets?"

"No! Mom, I swear to you I didn't. I'm telling you the truth when I say that someone else is posing as me and trying to get me in trouble."

"Sweetie...do you know who it could be? Does anyone hate you so much that they would want this to happen to you?"

"I don't think so mom."

"Because if you even have the faintest idea as to who might be behind this, you need to tell me, so we can tell the police. Then the police will start looking into the other person and maybe you'll escape from this entire mess unscathed."

"I know, mom," Angela sighed. "I promise you, I will tell you the minute I think of someone who might want to do something like this to me, but right now, I swear to you that I don't know anything."

Mrs. Hernandez gave her daughter a hug. "Don't worry, sweetie. We'll sort this out."

Later on in the day, Angela decided to get out of the house for a while. She walked down the street, enjoying the fresh air. There was a gentle breeze blowing and it ruffled through her hair. Angela took a minute to think about what had been happening over the last few days, about how quickly something that had seemed amazing had gone downhill. *I guess it was too good to be true,* she thought. Suddenly, Angela realized what she hadn't done that she should have. She hadn't been to visit Rose yet.

Angela entered the hospital holding a bouquet of flowers and walked across the marble floor, over to the reception table. "Excuse me," she said to the lady behind the table. "I'm here to visit Rose Evans."

"Ah, the Evans girl," the lady said, shuffling through papers. "She's a popular kid, she is. Has had a number of visitors over the last few days. A tragedy happened to her though, but it is a good thing she survived. Ah, here you are. She's been transferred out of the emergency ward to room 361. That's on the third floor, and elevators are that way," she pointed to the left.

Angela thanked the lady and walked to the elevators. She was joined by several other people, all heading to different floors. She was thankful that no one was going to see Rose, because then it would have been likely that they would recognize her as the girl who had caused Rose to end up in the hospital.

"What are you here for darling?" a nice, older lady asked Angela as she got into the lift. "A nice young girl like you shouldn't be spending time in the hospital."

"Um, I'm here to visit a friend," Angela replied quietly.

"Ah. Well, give my best wishes to your friend."

"Thank you. Give my best wishes to the person you're visiting too."

"I will do that."

The lift bell dinged, signalling that they had reached the third floor. Angela nodded to the lady and made her way out of the doors. She walked down and read the numbers on each door as she passed them, 356...358...360...361.

Angela stood outside Rose's door for a few minutes, because she almost got cold feet. Rose wouldn't want to see her, not after what she had done to her. Maybe coming here was a bad idea. What was she thinking anyway? Did she think that coming here and giving Rose flowers would make everything alright? She was about to walk away when the door opened and Diana came out of the room. She made eye-contact with Angela and glared at her, before walking away.

It was then that Angela remembered why she had come; she wanted to explain to Rose what had happened and to apologize. Although it wouldn't make things right, it would help her sleep a little better at night and this was something that she had to do. Taking a deep breath, Angela knocked on the door before pushing it open and entering.

Mrs. Evans saw Angela first and recognized her instantly. When someone does something harmful to a person that you care about, their image is forever emblazoned into your mind. You'll never forget their face, and whenever you see them, you'll want to punch them. You want them to never forget what they've done - the suffering they've caused. Mrs. Evans's face was set into a hard line. "You're not welcome here Angela. Please leave."

Rose looked up upon hearing the name Angela. She saw a girl standing opposite her mother, a girl with long brown hair and hazel eyes - just like Angela's. However, the girl didn't look like Angela. She didn't have the same expressions as Angela and didn't radiate the same aura as Angela. It seemed as if she had changed.

"I'm sorry Mrs. Evans," Angela began. "I just wanted to stop by and see how Rose was doing."

"See how she was doing!? Alright, well, she's doing fine. She's doing fine after you almost killed her!"

"Mom," Rose said quietly. "That's not fair."

"Not fair? Rose, have you forgotten what she wrote?"

"No, but she wasn't the only one who was bullying me. There were other people too. She may be the one who drove me over the edge, but I don't think she's fully to blame."

"I wanted to apologize too and explain," Angela continued.

"Explain? Explain what?" Mrs. Evans clearly wanted to get rid of Angela as soon as she possibly could. In her eyes, Angela had done far more harm than good.

"Please. Listen." Angela began to explain everything. She told Rose and Mrs. Evans the same things that she had told her parents, and the police. They listened attentively and Angela tried to judge whether or not they believed her through their facial expressions. However, she'd never been particularly good at reading people and this time was no exception. She had no idea what they were thinking or whether they believed her, but she still continued to talk. Regardless of whether or not they were convinced by her story, she wanted to know for herself that she had told them the absolute truth.

Upon finishing her story, Angela looked straight at Rose. "I'm sorry Rose. I may not have sent that tweet, but this is my fault. Two weeks ago, I had the power to stop that person, but I made a stupid decision. I cared more about popularity. I should have never let that account continue and because of this, my judgement backfired on me. Now look at me. Everyone hates me and most importantly, I've had my identity stolen. I've lost control of my life and something that I didn't do is going to go on my permanent record. It's going to haunt me for the rest of my life, but worst of all, my decision end up hurting you. You almost died because of me and I am so very sorry. I don't expect you to forgive me, but I do hope that one day, maybe you will."

The room was filled with silence. Mrs. Evans and Rose were processing what they had just heard and deciding whether or not to believe it, whether or not to forgive this girl. However, such decisions cannot be made in the space of two minutes. Sometimes, they can take years.

It was Mrs. Evans who finally spoke. "Angela...thank you for coming, but I think you should leave."

Angela nodded. "Thank you for listening to me." She left the flowers on Rose's bedside. "These are for you," she said quietly. "I'm very sorry, and I hope you get better. If there's anything I can do, please let me know." With those final words, she left.

Mrs. Evans turned to Rose. "Do you believe her?"

Rose continued looking straight ahead. "I'm not sure, but I think I do."

Chapter 15

The next morning, Angela was awoken by the sound of the doorbell. Her parents had agreed to let her stay home for another day and she was hoping to sleep in, as the exhaustion of the past few weeks had finally caught up with her. However, she was brought to consciousness by an annoying, loud ringing and she pulled her pillow over her ears, but was soon woken up by her mother.

"Angela. We need to talk."

Angela came downstairs, still in her pyjamas and her dressing gown. Her mother was sitting on the sofa and she did not look pleased. Next to her were stacks of cardboard boxes, Angela wondered what was going on.

"Mom..."

"Sit down Angela."

Angela sat down on the leather chair, next to the sofa. She kept eyeing the boxes curiously, wondering what was in them.

"Yesterday, you were there when I received the bill."

"The credit card bill? The odd one, with things on it that you hadn't ordered? Yeah, I was there. I told you the company must have made a mistake, since you didn't actually order any of those things."

"Well, it turns out that we actually did order the things." Mrs. Hernandez picked up the bill, from where it was lying next to her and handed it to Angela. She then began to open the boxes, taking out products that ranged from books and DVD's, to clothes and accessories. Angela was able to find each product that her mother took out from the boxes on the bill.

"I don't get it," Angela said. "We didn't order any of these things. Did the shipping company make a mistake too?"

"No," Mrs. Hernandez turned to look at Angela. "The delivery person said that all of these things were ordered by 'Angela Hernandez'."

"What?" Angela looked shocked. "But I didn't order these things!"

"Stop lying, Angela!" Mrs. Hernandez exclaimed, causing Angela to tremble. "The proof is there. You abused the trust that your father and I put in you when we allowed you to use our credit card. We said with permission, but you clearly didn't understand that. You must have snuck in and gotten it from our room."

"No! I didn't!"

"Then how are these packages here? Why did the delivery person say you ordered them? Do you have an explanation for that!?" Angela was silent. "You know, I didn't think that you would do something like this and then lie about it. Did you lie about the Twitter account as well? Are you really behind it?"

"What!? Mom, no! I'm not. I've already told you that."

"I don't know if I can trust you anymore."

Angela ran upstairs into her room and slammed the door. She could bet that the person who had ordered the things in her name, was the same person who had set up the Twitter account. Someone was sabotaging her and had stolen her identity away from her. She had no control left over her life and it felt horrible. She didn't know what to do anymore. No one trusted her. No one believed her. She was stuck in a position where she really was all alone.

She had read about identity theft in the newspaper, however, the reporter had always given an objective view of the subject. She hadn't realized how it felt when someone steals your identity. It felt horrible. In this world, the only thing she could ever be sure of was that she was who she was. She could be sure of her decisions. Now, she wasn't making the choices in her own life anymore. She had been completely thrown.

Chapter 16

The police had come to know about the incident with the credit card. Detective Stevens racked it up to the idea that Angela was a troublemaker who didn't know where to stop. As it was the credit card of Angela's parents, no criminal charges could be pressed against her. However, Angela had completely lost the trust of her parents. They, who had believed her from the very beginning, now found themselves doubting her story.

Detective Stevens and Detective Randall had spent time interviewing students from Angela's school, in order to get a better idea of what she was like. They had then decided that if the case was to move any further and if they were going to find Angela guilty of cyber-bullying, they would need to get some solid evidence against her. They needed something that explicitly said she had been the one who had sent the tweet, but there had been no evidence, no witnesses, nothing. Detective Randall thought that perhaps they'd be able to get evidence if they confiscated the Hernandez's family's laptops. That way, they could look at the browser history and other such things.

Detective Stevens managed to get a warrant for the laptops of Clara Hernandez, Richard Hernandez and Angela Hernandez. Mr. and Mrs. Hernandez were not too pleased about having their laptops taken away, calling the measure "unnecessary". However, the police wanted to cover all their bases and the chances that Angela had been using her parents' laptops was very possible.

They took the laptops over to the tech department and spent the day there checking each computer's browser history. Mr. and Mrs. Hernandez's laptops didn't have any evidence of Twitter or recent Amazon access, which was the website that Angela had ordered the things from. They then tried Angela's laptop. Twitter had been accessed, but it wasn't the homepage. Angela had gone onto her own Twitter page several times, but according to her history, she had never logged into the website. As for Amazon, there was no record of her accessing the website in the last three months. They went through her trash too, in case she had deleted the history, but had forgotten to get rid of it completely.

"She probably double-deleted the history," Detective Stevens said. "It's what I would do if I was in her situation. Plus the kids these days are awfully tech-savvy. She'd know that she'd have to delete the history from the trash as well if she wanted to get rid of it completely."

"Yeah," Detective Randall said, although he seemed to be lost in thought.

A uniformed officer entered the room. "Detective Stevens, a student from San Christo High is here to see you as requested. A Cassandra Jones."

Detective Stevens got up. "Coming, Randall?"

"Uh, no sir, I think I'll stay here. Continue working on the computers and see if I can find anything."

"You're on to something, aren't you?"

"I think I may be, sir, but I'm not really quite sure yet."

"Alright Randall, suit yourself. We've interviewed so many students that we're probably not going to get any more new information. You're likely to be of more use here than you will be in my office."

"My sentiments exactly, sir."

Detective Stevens and the uniformed officer walked out, leaving Randall alone in the tech room. He kept staring at Angela's browser history. Something was off, but he wasn't quite sure what it was yet. Then it hit him. If Angela had wanted to delete the history of her accessing Twitter on her laptop, she would have probably run a search on the history page of her browser and deleted every mention of Twitter that came up. The question was, why were the frequent visits to the Twitter page itself still there? Why didn't she delete those as well? She would have wanted to distance herself from the account as much as possible and therefore wouldn't have left a single link to any page associated with Twitter on her history.

Detective Randall was the kind of cop who fully invested in his cases. He had done pretty well in both school and university, but had chosen to become a cop because he wanted to make the world a better place. A maor part of making the world a better place was making sure that no one got wrongfully convicted. He wanted to be sure that who he arrested was guilty. Right now, he was not at all sure that Angela Hernandez was guilty.

Suddenly, an idea dawned on him. He took his cell phone out of his pocket and dialled the number of his friend, Jason, who was a tech consultant. He had worked with the Edmonton Police Department before and Detective Randall felt that his expertise was needed in this case.

"Hello?" Jason said, when he picked up.

"Hi Jason! I'm calling on business. I assume you're familiar with the Angela Hernandez case?"

"The one about the girl who was sending mean tweets to others and made another girl try to kill herself? Yep. News travels fast in this town. Why, what's up?"

"I have reason to believe that Angela's not guilty," Detective Randall proceeded to explain the issue of the browser history, and the story that Angela had told the police about how someone had stolen her identity. Jason listened attentively.

"So, what do you need me to do?"

"I was wondering if you could trace the creation of the Twitter account, along with the online purchases that Angela allegedly made. I mean, I'm not even sure if it's possible..."

"It is. I'll be down at the police station at about 5 PM and we'll work on this then."

"Got it. Thanks Jason."

That evening, Jason arrived at the police station right on time. He was carrying a thin black laptop briefcase, containing his treasured MacBook Pro. Detective Randall was waiting to greet him. "Thanks for coming. Your skills are going to be a great help."

"No problem," Jason said, following Detective Randall into the tech room. He had been in there several times before, assisting the department whenever they needed any technical help. He was considered to be the foremost technological expert in Edmonton.

Sitting down at a table, Jason unpacked his computer, opened it up and logged on. "Okay, so you want to track the creation of a Twitter account? Angela Hernandez's account, I'm assuming?"

Detective Randall nodded. "That's correct. I want to know which computer the account was created from and who's been logging into the account. It's likely that if we find the computer that's logging into the account, the owner will be the person who's really sending out the tweets."

"Okay. What I need to do here is track the IP address. That's like a unique set of numbers that each computer has. Every time someone logs into an account, or even just uses the Internet on that computer, that string of numbers is sent to the server. We can extract the IP address used to log onto Angela's account, and then track it. We can find out which computer that IP address belongs to. It sounds simple, but it's quite difficult in reality, and it's a fairly lengthy process."

"Well, I'm glad we have you then," Detective Randall smiled. "Let's get to work."

It took Jason around an hour to pinpoint the IP address. While he was working, he liked to talk. He asked

Randall a series of questions about the case, as he was rather curious as to why Randall was investigating further when it seemed rather clear that Angela Hernandez was behind everything. "Anyone can make up a story, Carson," he said as he typed furiously. "I'll admit, her story was relatively detailed, but she could have just improvised or even prepared it before-hand."

"Something just doesn't seem right," Detective Randall replied. "Yes, it seems to be her. If I was someone else, I would probably be certain that it was Angela because that's how it appears on the surface. However, as a detective, I have to look beneath the surface. If Angela gets charged, it'll go on her permanent record, and it will negatively affect her. I want to be completely sure that she's guilty before something like that happens."

"You're something else, Carson," Jason shook his head, smiling. "Most people would just say that Angela did it and leave it at that. They'd be too lazy to go any deeper. It helps me sleep better at night knowing that there are still people like you left in this world."

Soon after their conversation, Jason managed to pinpoint and track the IP address. "The computer, that was used to create the account and has been logging into the account, is located around the Rosebury Drive area."

"But that's at the West end of town," Detective Randall said, surprised. "Angela Hernandez lives at the East end of town."

"Well, it looks like Angela's not your girl. Every single time this Twitter account has been logged into, it's been logged into from the same computer. Hold on, I'm just finding out who it's registered to," Jason began to type again. "Hmm. It's registered to a Mr. Clark Somerset."

"Somerset..." Detective Randall thought out loud. "I've heard that name before. Yes! That's right! Angela goes to school with a girl named Diana Somerset. Apparently, Angela has never been particularly nice to Diana; in fact, she's been quite the opposite."

"That's motive," Jason nodded.

"Can you track the online purchases in a similar manner to the way you tracked the Twitter account?" Detective

Randall asked. "Find out which computer made the purchases?"

"I can do that. Most online shopping websites track the IP addresses of their customers, in case a situation like this emerges."

Half an hour later, Jason had managed to get the IP address. It was an exact match to the address of the computer used to create and log into the Twitter account. It appeared that Diana could very well be the person who had stolen Angela's identity.

Detective Stevens entered the tech room. "Randall! What are you still doing here? And Jason? I didn't know you were coming in today!"

"Sir," Randall began. "We've got something that you're going to want to see. We decided to trace the creation of the Twitter account. The computer used to create and log into the Twitter account is not registered to Angela Hernandez. In fact, it is registered to a Mr. Clark Somerset; the father of one of Angela's classmates, Diana Somerset. We also traced the online purchases allegedly made by Angela to the same computer."

"Very interesting, Randall," Stevens looked impressed. "There's clearly someone else involved here and Diana does have a motive. The girl I interviewed earlier today, Cassandra, says that Diana was Angela's main target. She also says that a couple of days before Angela's meanness on Twitter was initiated, she had a public falling out with Diana. They were put together for some project and Angela refused to do any of the work, so Diana did it all."

"That's not just motive, that's excellent timing," Randall commented.

"Exactly. But one question remains: how did Diana manage to get the credit card number that she would have needed to make the purchases?"

"I've been thinking that too, sir and I've come up with a theory. I'm not sure whether it's true or not, but it is plausible. Jason, if you'll excuse me," Randall went to the computer and typed in the web address for Facebook. He logged into his own account and then ran a search for "Angela Hernandez". Narrowing the search down through location, he found her almost immediately. He clicked on her profile.

"Nearly everything here is public," he said. "Anyone can see it." He clicked on her friends list and searched for Diana. "Diana's not her friend on Facebook, but that doesn't matter. She could still see all of the information on Angela's wall. That's probably how she found out enough about her to properly impersonate her on Twitter."

"Kids these days," Stevens shook his head. "Don't they understand how dangerous the internet is?"

"Clearly not," Randall had scrolled down Angela's timeline until he reached his goal. A picture of Angela's parents' credit card, with the numbers engraved clear. "That's how Diana got the card numbers."

"Good work Randall," Stevens clapped him on the back. "Angela might actually have had her identity stolen. She might have been telling the truth. We'll need to check that computer out. I'll call up the judge's office and get a warrant. We'll go over there tomorrow morning and it's Saturday, so the girl will be at home. In the meantime, keep this quiet. We don't need her to find out about this and delete her history.

"Yes sir."

Chapter 17

The very next morning, Detective Stevens, Detective Randall and Jason paid the Somersets a visit. Detective Stevens had gone to the judge's office the previous night and had managed to get a warrant, which allowed him to check out all of the computers in the home.

The detectives arrived outside Diana's house and rang the doorbell. A man opened the door.

"Mr Clark Somerset?" Detective Stevens asked.

"Yes," the man answered.

"You're the father of Diana Somerset?"

"Yes, what is this about?"

Detective Stevens held up his badge. "I'm Detective Stevens and this is Detective Randall. We're from the Edmonton Police Department, and we're handling the Angela Hernandez case. This is Jason, he's consulting with us for the technical aspect of this case."

"Yes, we're familiar with the case. Are you here to interview my daughter?"

"Actually, we have reason to believe that your daughter is more involved in this case than she's let on. May we please come in?"

"Of course," Mr. Somerset moved aside to let the detectives in. He was rather confused. He'd already asked Diana whether she knew anything about the case and she had said that she didn't really know much.

Mr. Somerset led the detectives into the family's living room. There were three people gathered around the TV, a woman who the detectives presumed to be Diana's mother, along with Diana and Sofia. "Detectives, this is my wife, Elizabeth, and this is my older daughter, Sofia. You already know Diana. Girls, this is Detective Stevens, Detective Randall, and their consulting tech expert, Jason. They're here about the Angela Hernandez case."

"Detectives," Mrs. Somerset stood up and shook their hands. "Can I get you some tea, coffee, anything to drink?"

"That's very kind of you, but no thank you," Detective Stevens answered. "Actually, we're here to talk about your daughter Diana." Diana looked up, surprised.

"Oh," Mrs. Somerset looked surprised. "Are you here to interview Diana? I've heard that you've been interviewing students from the school?"

"We're not here to interview her. As I mentioned to your husband at the door, we believe that Diana may be more involved in this case than she has let on. You see, Angela Hernandez told us that it wasn't her behind the Twitter account; that she had had her identity stolen. Now, we didn't believe her at the time, but as police detectives, it is our job to look into everything so that we're sure that we're convicting the right person."

Detective Randall took over then. "So we traced the IP address of the computer that was used to create the Twitter account and has been used to log into the account. We also traced the IP address of the computer that was used to make multiple online purchases from Angela's Hernandez's parents' credit card. The addresses matched and they were from a computer that was registered to you, Mr. Somerset."

"I don't understand," Mr. Somerset said.

"Mr. Somerset, how many computers do you have in your possession?"

"Four. Mine, my wife's, Diana's, and Sofia's."

"Are they all registered in your name?"

"I believe so."

"Mr. Somerset, we'd like to see Diana's computer. We believe that she may have stolen Angela's identity and may be the one behind the Twitter account. We aren't sure, and therefore we have to see her computer and browser history in order to prove her guilt or innocence."

"Hold on," Mrs. Somerset stopped the detectives. "You've got to have some legal document permitting you to take possession of private property."

"We do," Detective Stevens held up the warrant. "It allows us to check all of your computers. Mr. Somerset, could you please bring us Diana's computer?"

Mr. Somerset got up to get the laptop. Everyone else, including Diana, remained silent. When he got back, he handed the laptop to Jason and didn't say a word. Jason opened up the laptop. He asked Diana to input her password, and she did, silently. He then opened her browser history and began to search through it. Surely enough, Twitter appeared frequently throughout the history, with login pages and dashboards. Jason opened the Twitter homepage and typed in Angela's username in the login box. He clicked away, and a password appeared, showing that the password for Angela's login had been saved. Also in the history were visits to the Amazon pages of the things that Angela had allegedly ordered, as well as several visits to Angela's Facebook page. Jason looked grimly at Detective Stevens and Detective Randall. This didn't look good for Diana.

"Diana, we have just found multiple visits to Twitter in your browser history. You also have the password to the Twitter account that allegedly belongs to Angela Hernandez and is in her name saved on your browser. There are also visits to the Amazon pages of the products allegedly ordered by Angela Hernandez and several visits to Angela's Facebook page. I'm afraid you're going to have to come with us down to the police station."

"Diana?" Mrs. Somerset turned to look at her younger daughter, shocked. "Did you do this?"

"No!" Diana shouted. "No, I swear I didn't. Someone set me up, I didn't do it!"

"I'm sorry Diana," Detective Stevens said. "But the evidence is against you right now. Please come with us. Mr. and Mrs. Somerset, as Diana is a minor, you'll need to accompany us."

"I didn't do anything!" Diana said again. "It wasn't me."

"Look, Diana, the browser history is there. You had the password saved on your computer!"

"No, stop," this time, the voice was different. Sofia had stood up and was facing the detectives. "She didn't do it. It was me. I'm the one who's guilty. Diana had nothing to do with it, I just used her computer. It was all me."

The Somerset family was in Detective Stevens's office. Sofia hadn't said a word as they got into the car, saying that she would only speak once they were at the police station. Detective Stevens and Detective Randall entered the room and sat down, behind the desk. "Alright Sofia. We're listening. Why did you do it?"

Sofia sighed and looked around. "I didn't like the way Angela was treating my sister. Diana's new to this town, and I know how hard it is to start a new school. She didn't have any friends and was struggling. She didn't tell me at first, but I could see it, but then she told me about how that girl had refused to work with her for the science project they had been assigned to work on together. Diana was so hurt by the way that she spoke to her! I couldn't believe that someone could be so arrogant. So, I took matters into my own hands. I went through Angela's Facebook profile and got tons of information on her. I then created the Twitter account. I just wanted her to pay a little bit and feel what it was like to have no friends at all, like Diana. That was my primary aim. I felt a bit guilty at first, but then, Diana handed in the project that she had slaved on all weekend giving Angela credit even though that girl hadn't laid a finger on the poster. She didn't even appreciate that! I felt justified about what

I was doing, but the account backfired, and she became more popular! When she became more popular, she started torturing my sister even more and I felt horrible, because I knew that I was the reason that Angela was being so horrible to my sister. So I decided that if I sent a tweet to someone really sensitive, they'd take it to heart and do something extreme. Then Angela would be blamed, and no one would want to be around her. A friend of mine has a sister who goes to their school and used to be friends with Rose. I heard her talking about her one day and figured that Rose would be the perfect target. I never thought that she'd try to kill herself! But Angela did indeed get less popular and end up with no friends. I began to love how much control I had over her life and that was why I used the credit card. I decided I wanted to make sure that not one person in this town trusted her, ever again. I never planned to admit that I was responsible for all of these things, and it seemed that no one would ever suspect me anyway, as it seemed so obvious that Angela was at fault. However, when you detectives came to our house and thought it was Diana, I had to speak up. I couldn't have my baby sister taking the blame for something that I did. I never should have used her laptop in the first place. The only reason I used it was because what I did had to be done quickly. My laptop is slow and useless, while Diana's was quicker and easier to use. That's the only reason I used it."

"Sofia, you're over eighteen, aren't you?" Detective Stevens asked. Sofia nodded, tearfully. "Unfortunately, this is going to have some horrible consequences for you. Not only will you be charged with a misdemeanor of cyber-harassment, you'll also be charged for identity theft and credit card fraud. You could go to jail for as long as thirty years, but since you've cooperated, I'll put a good word in with the judge."

"I'm so sorry," Sofia said, beginning to cry.

Chapter 18

By Sunday, everyone knew that it was Sofia who was behind the account. People reacted to the news in different ways; some had gone and apologized to Angela for treating her badly, while others accused her of being a fake. Angela graciously accepted the apologies and ignored the name-calling. Through this incident, she had grown up. She no longer cared about popularity and she also now protected her Facebook account. She had gone and apologized to every single person who she had been mean to.

Rose was up and back on her feet. She attended school and found herself thrust into the spotlight. Many people had approached her to tell her that they were there for her if she ever needed it, and apologized for the way they had treated her in the past. Angela also spoke to Rose, apologizing again for the trouble that she had caused her. Rose forgave her, graciously saying that it wasn't really her fault and that if she was in Angela's position, she would have probably done the same thing.

At lunch, Angela was welcomed back at her old table. She invited Rose to come and sit with them, and she accepted. Angela had come to learn that Rose was indeed a very nice person. In the years to come, they would become close friends.

Around halfway through lunch, Diana came up to Angela and Rose and asked if she could speak to them privately. They agreed, and moved to a quieter and more secluded area.

"I just wanted to say sorry on behalf of my sister," Diana began, looking at the ground. "I wanted to apologize from my side too. Sofia would have never done those things if it wasn't for me. I'm sorry that you two had to suffer so much. Angela, you might have said some mean things to me in the past, but that's nothing compared to what happened to you. You almost got charged with something that you didn't doand Rose, you could have died because of what Sofia said. I'm sorry for ignoring you every time you tried to be nice to me too. The truth is, I was insecure."

"I'm sorry too, Diana," Angela took Diana's hands in hers. "I'm really sorry for everything I said to you. If I could take it all back, I would."

Diana smiled. Many years later, these three girls would still be in touch. They were brought together by a negative incident, but had moved on, forming a close friendship. They never had forgotten what had happened, but each of them had grown from it, learning valuable life lessons. They would never make the same mistakes again.

-The End-

www.ingramcontent.com/pod-product-compliance
Lightning Source LLC
Chambersburg PA
CBHW070508200726
48293CB00007B/2448